Feverish Dream

Chapter 1

Daniel Tale stepped out of his apartment, needing to go on a walk to contemplate everything which had happened that day. It felt surreal to him. So much had changed in a day. A *single* day. It was hard to fathom. So hard to fathom, in fact, that he'd constantly had a confused and frustrated look on his face since the last, big change- a change which had occurred only a few minutes before.

Daniel trotted down the stairs and pushed through the door of his apartment building, knocking his left shoulder on the door as he opened it, only proving to himself that he was possibly too distracted to have an entirely safe journey.

After jumping down the four, concrete steps which led to the front door, Daniel pushed through the gate and turned to the right, heading for a park which he liked to jog around in the mornings. He found it calming as it was large and barren enough to allow for him to completely shield himself from the world while jogging on the path which led through a small forest. He'd very rarely see anyone there, something which made it seem like the perfect place to go to contemplate his unfortunate day of events.

Daniel tried to push the memories away

alongside everything which came with them: fear, sadness, doubt, worry, anxiety, uncertainty and, most of all, confusion. He didn't want to deal with anything, not even a single, depressing thought or reminder, until he'd be walking on the trail which he so desperately wanted to be travelling down.

After travelling for a minute or two and crossing a busy road, having had to wait for a few moments for the abundance of vehicles to dissipate and allow him to continue his journey, Daniel took a turn to the right, beginning to walk on the slightly-damp, dirt path which greeted everyone who walked into the park. The path was almost sticky as it had been drizzling rain not long before, something which seemed extremely appropriate when considering how Daniel was feeling.

The forest wasn't very far away, maybe only a few hundred metres, but Daniel felt as if the journey would take hours just to get close to it. He couldn't hold everything back for much longer. It was beginning to seep through his mental barriers as they fought to keep the restraints as strong as possible, slowly tiring with every second, occasionally letting the restraints slip away for a moment, allowing a painful jab of thought to attack Daniel's mind until the barrier could regain its grip on the restraints and hold the memories, thoughts and feelings back. They needed to be a safe distance away from his mind. Just for a little longer. Then they could spew out and overwhelm him as much as they craved. Daniel accepted that he was going to be pained for a while, but he knew that he couldn't let everything build up. He'd done it once before in high school, holding back copious amounts of stress, anxiety and worry, only fuelling an unhealthy fire which he didn't realise was blazing until it was almost too late.

It was nearing. The opening to the maze of trees was getting close enough that Daniel could almost smell the calming stench of damp bark. Just for a little longer. Just for a tiny bit longer, then he'd let it out. There were only fifty or so metres between him and the first tree. Maybe it was time to let the restraints go…

Laura. The pain which she'd caused him. It was almost too much to feel it again, to feel the stabbing agony of knowing that, for months, maybe even an entire *year*, she hadn't loved him. She'd admitted it. She'd blatantly admitted it alongside the confession that she'd been seeing other men for months. *Men. Months.* Multiple people, maybe for as long as half of a year. How had she decided not to let slip what was going on? How had she managed to trick him for so long, to feed him exactly what he wanted only to rip it away so suddenly that he was left dazed and stunned with no idea as to what to do next? She'd been his girlfriend since their first year of university. She'd been his girlfriend for six years. *Six* years, with the last one probably having been spent with a myriad of other men alongside him. How? *How*? It seemed ridiculous. It seemed like some sort of film plot, but Daniel knew that he wasn't in a film. He knew that he wasn't in some type of story. He was suffering. *Actually* suffering. How much had he done for her over the years? Over the first three, probably about as much as anyone would expect from a partner. But for the last three? Daniel knew that he'd gone above and beyond all expectations. He'd slacked off of his Biochemistry work in university just because she'd wanted to spend more time with him. Doing so had resulted in him failing the subject, it resulted in him being stuck, a giant roadblock in the way of the road which led to his dream career. His *dream* career. He'd thrown the chance away just for her. And how did she repay him? By sleeping with a flurry of other men a year later.

What hurt Daniel the most about it was that she'd been happy that morning. He'd left for work- he'd left for that stupid job which he didn't even like- and she'd kissed him, she'd wished him to have a good day- which was ironic given that she'd probably been planning to ruin his year at that point- and she'd told him that she had a surprise for him when he'd get home. When Daniel had heard that, he'd thought that they'd have a homemade dinner date, that they'd have a movie night, that she'd invited some of his friends around so they could all have fun together, hang out as they only had a proper chance to every few months. What had the surprise been? "Um, Daniel. Just so you know, I stopped loving you a long time ago, I've been cheating on you for a few months, and I'm moving out. Bye! Have fun being alone and upset!" Of course, that hadn't been how Laura had broken the news to him. She'd done so probably as gently as she possibly could have, but Daniel didn't remember it as gentle. He remembered it

4

as if she'd held a giant butcher's knife and had brandished it proudly, had pointed it at him and had broken the news in the harshest way possible while making him fear for his life. It genuinely felt as if she'd *ended* his life. Well, that alongside the other two things which had happened.

Daniel stopped walking, his arms stretched out, leaning against the tree. He hadn't realised it, but he'd already travelled a third of the way down the route. He'd been thinking for a while, trying to accept what had happened. He'd been struggling. A lot. He felt as if he was going to throw up. He was almost retching while pushing against the tree as if doing so would keep the gagging at bay. He felt ill. Tremendously ill. He almost felt as if he'd eaten a bad meal but, of course, the only thing which he'd eaten which had been bad had been a forkful of uncertainty and sorrow.

After taking a moment to compose himself, Daniel stood up straight, let out a long sigh, then turned to keep walking. He was in his favourite part of the walk. There was a river flowing nearby, just through the trees on the left and, because the area was usually so vacant, Daniel could hear the water flowing, a constant trickle as the river flowed towards somewhere where he hadn't explored yet. It amplified the tranquillity of the area, allowing for him to calm down a little. Laura had left him. She hadn't loved him for a while. She'd cheated on him. Daniel knew that he just had to accept it. He wanted her back, of course. He still loved her even though what she'd confessed had been heart-wrenching for him. He still loved her, nonetheless, but knew that there wasn't any point in chasing after her. He knew that running after her, trying to find her and making her give him another chance to make up for the one which he hadn't realised had been his last was pointless. He'd just end up hurting himself more in the future if she decided to take him back. It would be healthier for him to just let go.

Daniel stopped walking again, halting his tracks, his eyes closed. He tried to imagine the good things which would come to his life without Laura being in it. He'd spend less money every month as he'd only be feeding himself and he wouldn't have to pay for fancy nights out in restaurants which were almost too expensive for him to afford in the first place. He wouldn't have to worry about balancing a work life and a normal life. He could tip his focus more towards his work for a while and get much more stable. Well, that was required anyway. Given that he'd also been fired from his job, he didn't have a choice but to focus as hard as possible on finding another stable occupation.

That was another which had happened that day. After Daniel had watched Laura leave the apartment with two suitcases and a promise to collect the rest of her things the next day, Daniel had sat on the side of his bed, staring at the floor, trying to process everything. He'd had the urge to just go on the walk then, but he couldn't find the strength which he needed to do so. He simply sat on the side of the bed, trying not to think about how that bed was now solely his and not shared

6

with Laura anymore. He tried so desperately for so long to distract himself or convince himself that he was okay and that everything would work out in the end.

While Daniel had been trying to get over the fact that Laura had just left him, trying to force himself to hate her given what she'd done, thinking that it would make it easier to get over the girl which he still, for some reason, craved, his phone had begun ringing. After picking it up, Daniel had been barraged by his boss, being shouted at as his boss had found a clump of marijuana in Daniel's desk. Even though Daniel had insisted that it wasn't his, even though he'd explained that the only time he'd ever smoked weed had been once in university and that he only smoked cigarettes, his boss didn't want to hear anything about it.

Given that Daniel's heart had been broken only a few dozen minutes before, Daniel found it increasingly difficult to dispute his boss' claims. He processed that, according to his boss, his co-workers had all been proved to have been clear of being connected to the drug, confusing him even more, but Daniel just couldn't bring himself to keep up his defence. He was fired over the phone, told to pick his stuff up from the office the next day otherwise it would all be binned, but Daniel didn't couldn't even *think* about going to that office building again. One of his co-workers had clearly hidden the drug in his desk, then had managed to get Daniel fired as a result. He didn't want to go back to the building and have to see everyone look at him, probably believing that he *was* the owner of the drug, and he *definitely* didn't want to go back and have to wonder about who *really* owned the drug.

Daniel stopped walking, frustrated. He closed his eyes and tried to calm himself down with a few deep breaths. If he could find out which one of the people whom he used to be acquainted with had blamed him... No. Daniel didn't want to punch them. Well, actually, he did, but he didn't want to have to deal with any charges for assault alongside everything else. He'd already had a tough-enough day. Being dumped, being fired, being told that his family cat of eighteen years had been run over...

Normally, Daniel wouldn't have cried at the news. He would have been upset, but he wouldn't have cried. The cat was old, anyway. It was due to die of old age within a few months, probably, but he hadn't had the time to properly accept that it was going to happen. Normally, Daniel would have realised that the end of the pet's life was approaching, and he would have spent time going over it, allowing for him to be much less affected when the time would arrive. But, given that the cat had been hit by a car and killed so suddenly when, obviously, no-one had expected the event to happen, Daniel had felt stunned to hear the news when his mother had phoned to tell him that evening. It had been strange. It had been the last straw which had made him decide to leave his apartment and go for a walk.

Daniel continued to walk in silence until he looked up and realised that he was about to walk right out of the park. He'd zoned out in a weird way, his legs still taking him in the right direction even though his brain hadn't been focused on the journey. The journey was already over and he had to return home.

Daniel walked out of the park and began heading back in the direction of his apartment. At least it wasn't far. It wouldn't take him very long to get home. Then, once he'd get there, he'd probably just go straight to bed. He hadn't eaten since lunch, but he wasn't hungry. Having so much happen to him in such a small space of time had taken a toll on his appetite. He probably wouldn't feel hungry until breakfast the next day, or maybe even later.

Daniel passed underneath a streetlamp as he pondered what he was going to do the next day. He'd been dumped and he'd been fired. It wasn't as if he could stay at home with Laura and get advice from her. It wasn't as if he could just go into work and distract himself by working twice as hard as usual. All distractions had been taken from him. He hadn't even told his mother yet despite the fact that she'd phoned him, having been overwhelmed by the piling-up of terrible events and having been scared that she'd end up babying him through the ordeal. If anything, too, he also just wanted to be alone. He'd needed some fresh air, and he'd managed to get some by taking a walk through the park. Now, he just needed sleep. Maybe that was what he'd do the next day: sleep.

A few shouts came from close by. Daniel expected that they were people on their way for a night out with some friends but, upon glancing down the street where the shouts had originated from, Daniel realised that it was a fight, practically in the middle of the road.

For a moment, Daniel debated what to do. Could he call the police? No, it probably wasn't serious enough to render the police necessary. Would it be a good idea to intervene? Well, there was always the chance that one of them was armed with a weapon of some sort. Daniel didn't want to end his misery-filled day with a trip to the hospital because he'd been stabbed in the stomach by a probably drunk idiot.

Daniel shook his head lightly and began crossing the road. They were a fair-few paces away from him. He wouldn't be roped into the ordeal. There wasn't any reason why he would-

Thud. Crash!

Daniel spun around after having just reached the other side of the road. The two people who'd been fighting were on their sides on the road, unmoving, alongside a totalled motorbike and the rider.

Daniel rushed over and almost gagged at the sight. The two people who'd been fighting were unconscious, one with a broken arm, the other with a broken leg. That wasn't what bothered Daniel the most, however. What got to him was the fact that the motorbike rider hadn't been wearing a helmet- or it hadn't been tightened properly and had flown off upon the collision- and, as a result, the rider had slammed his head into the tarmac, having cracked his skull open, copious amounts of blood oozing from the wound.

Daniel thought that the man even looked slightly familiar for some reason. He had short, brown hair and light, brown eyes which were wide with the shock of having flown off his bike and into the ground, though, even though his eyes were open, he was unconscious. Maybe dead. He was fairly tall, but not too far off the average height. He didn't look like any of Daniel's friends, so he didn't know why he looked familiar. Maybe he'd seen the man on TV, or something.

Daniel pulled his phone out and immediately phoned for an ambulance, explaining what had happened, detailing what was wrong with the three people. Then, once he'd hung up, Daniel walked away, heading for his apartment. He didn't want to have to wait around for the ambulances to arrive and then explain what had happened. He might have been a witness, at least to the extent where he knew what had been going on before the motorbike and the rider had arrived, but he didn't want to be one. After the day he'd had, he didn't want to end up having to stay around a possibly dead body.

After putting his phone back into his pocket, Daniel turned and continued walking home, trying to push the image of the rider's head out of his mind. Though, one thing which kept coming back to him, the thing which he couldn't escape no matter how hard he'd try, was that he *knew* that the man had died. He hadn't checked the rider's pulse, but with his head cracked open, with the amount of blood which had been gushing out of the wound, there wasn't any way that the man could have survived. If he *had* survived, Daniel would have simply assumed that he was a wizard and that he'd healed himself.

Daniel, while walking to his apartment, struggled to believe everything which had happened that day. Laura had left him. He'd been fired for, essentially, no reason. His long-term family pet had died. He might have witnessed a man die. How had all of that happened in a single day? Had just *one* of those things occurred, Daniel would have been upset, to say the least. Had two of those things happened, he would have probably considered it a fairly terrible day. But three? Four? Daniel could say without a doubt that it had been the worst day of his life. He even guessed that it was probably going to be the worst day of his *entire* life. So many terrible things had happened. What next? Had the awful luck run out? Would he enter his apartment to find that it was on fire? Would someone burgle him in the night? Would he be murdered? Would he receive a phone call from the police explaining that he was under suspicion for rigging the accident which had occurred? Would he be called into the hospital to visit someone he loved dearly? Daniel wasn't sure. He was almost petrified to find out. The last thing which he needed was for something else to happen. For anything bad to happen to him for the remainder of the day. What he needed was to somehow fix it all, to go back in time and stop it all from happening in the first place. Well, he'd let Laura go. She hadn't loved him for ages, anyway, so what was the point? But, aside from Laura, he'd make sure to find out who'd been hiding their weed in his desk, he'd make sure to call his parents and tell them to keep the cat inside, he'd made sure to warn the two people who had been fighting in the street that a motorbike was on its way. He'd do *anything* to change that day. But that wouldn't happen. Daniel knew that the existence of time travel was unlikely, Daniel knew that there wasn't the possibility of changing everything, but he definitely *wanted* to fix it all.

Daniel turned and walked through the gate, closing it behind him simply by slamming it behind him. He moved up the path, walked up the steps, opened the front door, then headed to the stairs. He almost feared walking back into the apartment. What if Laura had decided to pick up her stuff early? He didn't know if he'd be able to cope with seeing her again in the same day. But, regardless of how Daniel felt, he was going to have to see her the next day. He didn't have a choice when it came to that and, honestly, Daniel believed that it would be better to just have her collect her stuff and leave forever. The longer he'd have to gaze at her belongings, the madder he'd end up.

In went the key. Daniel unlocked the door, walked into the apartment, then saw that it was exactly the same as he'd left it.

"Okay," he muttered to himself. "No-one's waiting to kill me."

Daniel resisted the habit of calling out to Laura to tell her that he'd gotten back, something which he used to find himself doing even if he knew that she was at work or with friends or shopping. For the first time in two years, Daniel didn't call out upon entering the apartment. It felt strange. Daniel didn't like it.

The apartment was open-plan, basically the entirety of it combined into one room except for two bedrooms and the bathroom. Daniel had never cared for that detail but, now, he'd look anywhere and see reminders of everything which had disappeared from his life. The first, most obvious thing, was a picture of himself and Laura from a party which they'd attended in university. Another was the CV which Daniel kept on top of his desk in the far corner, having intended to use it to apply for a dozen other jobs as he'd never liked the one which he'd been fired from, though he ended up just sticking with it. Office work had never been the type of thing which Daniel had seen himself doing. He'd been studying to be a scientist in university, though he'd failed Biochemistry because Laura had wanted him to spend more time with her and he'd had to drop a lot of time which he should have spent revising to appease her. While in university, he'd worked as a waiter in a busy, local restaurant, and had enjoyed the experience thoroughly. It paid well, too. He'd ended up being fired from that job, too, however, as he'd ended up slacking off of work to catch up with the studying which he hadn't been doing. He'd lost the job and he'd lost his Biochemistry PhD.

Daniel kicked the wall, then yelped in pain. He hadn't broken a toe, but he'd managed to kick through the plasterboard which separated the entrance of the

14

apartment and the bathroom, and doing so hadn't been painless as his foot had been jabbed by a sharp dagger-like shard of plasterboard.

After kicking his shoes off, Daniel stormed to his bedroom. He needed sleep. He just needed sleep. That was all which he needed and all which he craved. Maybe he very slightly believed that the day had been a nightmare and that he'd simply wake up and everything would be fixed. Maybe he just hoped that his resentment and fear and anger would be gone by the morning. Whatever the incentive was, Daniel wanted to sleep.

He pulled his clothes off, trying to calm himself down, knowing that he wouldn't be able to sleep while worked-up. Then, once he was left in only his underwear, he slid underneath the covers, ignoring how cold the bed was.

Daniel's mind travelled back to the thought from earlier about changing everything which had gone wrong that day. He knew that it was pointless to think about and probably slightly unhealthy, but he began to ponder about what he'd change in regard to his entire life. If he could travel back in time, what would he change?

When thinking about it, Daniel could only think of a handful of things, some of them fairly obvious. For starters, he wouldn't substitute revision time for girlfriend time. That would get him his PhD and allow him to keep his old job. He'd also, if the event would still occur, make sure to warn the two people who'd been in the street, tell them to get out of the way. What else?

Daniel remained silent, his eyes closed, thinking until he heard he the sounds of two ambulances passing in front of his apartment, making him wince as the sound reminded his mind of the sight of the motorbike rider bleeding to death. He hoped that the man had survived against all odds but, of course, Daniel didn't doubt that his bad luck had caused the man to perish, making him feel slightly guilty even though it wasn't his fault. Though, maybe if he'd decided to intervene with the fight…

Daniel let out and annoyed noise and flipped onto his stomach, pressing his face into the pillow, trying to think about anything else which would distract him from the day's events and from the bad events of his life. He didn't want to continue thinking about what he'd change. It was probably unhealthy to do so. It would probably make him hate himself for choosing to do or not to do different things. The best thing which he could do was to force himself to sleep. Maybe he could focus on trying to force himself to sleep, then he'd magically fall unconscious? Maybe he could count sheep? Maybe he could simply think about nothing and hopefully shut his brain up? Maybe he could focus on relaxing each muscle of his body? Maybe he could imagine the feeling of being tired and somehow make the feeling a reality?

Daniel tried to myriad of different techniques, trying to get himself to fall unconscious. He was there for at least an hour, trying to force himself to fall asleep, until he flipped onto his back, let out a deep sigh, and just hoped that sleep would eventually overtake him. Maybe it was that he was trying too hard. Maybe it just had to be natural.

Whatever the cause, Daniel eventually fell asleep.

Chapter 2

Daniel's eyes fluttered open slowly as he processed that the alarm was beeping. He stuck his left arm out, looking for the alarm to turn it off, but his hand only contacted the duvet of his bed. He must have rolled over.

Daniel sidled towards the left side of the bed and allowed his eyes to adjust as he felt around for the alarm clock. No, that wasn't right. The sound was coming from his right, not his left. Why? He had his alarm clock on the left side of his bed.

The blurriness of Daniel's eyesight dissipated, making him begin to take in the room around him. His eyes first locked on the only poster in the room which hung on the wall opposite his bed, just next to the door. Then, his eyes drifted to the messy desk just underneath that, messy papers scattered on the surface. From there, he glanced at the TV; the painfully small screen which he'd had to resort to using. He wasn't in his bedroom. Where *was* he?

Daniel sat up quickly and stared around himself. The slightly rickety bedside table on the right side of his bed- with the alarm clock on top- which he could never even out because the floor was unreasonably uneven in that specific place. The chest of drawers which just

18

barely matched the colour of the rest of the furniture, slightly more tinted orange than the rest of the oak-coloured wood. He felt the mattress underneath himself, realising that it was the same one which had been left when he'd moved in. He was in his university dormitory.

After jumping out of bed, throwing the duvet back so violently that it fell off the other side of the double bed, Daniel silenced the alarm and then started to rush around the room, looking at every detail. The slight rip in the plain, light grey wallpaper behind the TV stand. The three-foot-tall mirror hanging on the wall which joined the corner to the doorframe, still in the dangerous position of possibly being smashed if someone were to open the door too violently. The single, long shelf which resided three feet above the head of the bed. It was true. He was in his university dorm room.

Daniel didn't know what to think. How was he back? Had he time travelled? He wasn't dreaming because he could remember all of the details about his life and he was *reacting* to the situation. What was going on?

Daniel took a few paces backwards and towards the door, confused, trying to figure it all out, when a thought hit him. A lucid dream. He'd heard about them before: a dream in which the dreamer is aware that they're seeing a fictitious scenario, but where they don't wake up as a result. He *was* dreaming. He was dreaming about the memory of his university life.

After turning to the left, intending to walk out of the room and see if his roommates were there, Daniel caught sight of himself in the mirror. He was the same as he'd been in his last year of university. He had his messy, black hair, a little frizzy as a result of being in his bed. His face was clean-shaven as opposed to the barely-grown beard which he had when in the real world. His hazel-coloured eyes stood out in comparison to the rest of his face as his hair was much longer than Daniel had grown used to, long enough to slightly obscure his eyesight when it was plastered to his forehead, crazily unkempt enough to almost make him look like a mad-scientist, complimenting the shade of his iris' very well.

Daniel almost smiled slightly. It felt strange to see a younger version of himself. It was almost as if he was reliving memories but with the ability to alter them… *Could* he alter them? Was there anything stopping him from going through a day in university while doing anything which he wanted? Could he run to Laura's dormitory, rush inside and punch her in the face without any consequences? Well, even if he *could*, Daniel wasn't going to. He wasn't a violent person. He wanted to have *some* revenge on Laura for destroying him, but that wasn't the right way to go about it. Anyway, what was to say that he wouldn't step out of his room and be greeted with somewhere completely different? Well, if he *was* having a lucid dream, he'd be able to make anything he wanted to happen *actually* happen. He'd be able to walk through that door and

20

force a wall to fall over with his mind. He could materialise a dinosaur into the living room and see what would happen. But, then again, did he even have the mental ability to do such a thing? Daniel guessed that he was only having a lucid dream about his last year in university because that was the year which he regretted the most in his life. The dream was built upon the foundation of memories. Would be really be able to drastically alter the dream without overloading his brain enough to force himself to wake up? Daniel didn't know and, when he considered the chances, he didn't want to risk it. He was back in university. Actually *back* in university. He could hang out with his friends, maybe get revenge on Laura for what she'd done to him, live his dream. He could fix the biggest of his regrets from the year and just see where his subconscious would take him. If it would happen to be a really long dream, he could graduate and finally have the satisfaction of being able to say that he'd survived university and graduated. He'd maybe be able to live his dream for a while if it would last for long enough. And, in all fairness, who was saying that it wouldn't last as long as he wanted? Daniel could technically live an entire lifetime in his head in the span of a single night. He *could* live his dream.

On the spot, Daniel made a decision. He decided that he was going to go through one day, then he'd see where that would lead. Maybe it would get really weird and he'd want to wake up. Maybe he'd end up getting really stressed by being back in university and would force himself to get out of the situation. But, at the very least, Daniel knew one thing: nothing which could happen could possibly be any worse than the day which he'd lived through.

Daniel took a step back from the mirror and gave an affirmative nod to himself, clarifying with himself that he was going to see what would happen if he'd change big things. He expected that the results would be interesting, at the very least.

After searching the floor of the room for the first clothes which he could find, Daniel pulled on a dark blue t-shirt and some black shorts, then bright green socks and his black, unbranded trainers. He took a moment to gaze at himself in the mirror, feeling very slightly narcissistic for doing so, but unable to believe that he was looking at a younger version of himself. It just seemed too unbelievable and insane. Daniel knew that the weirder part would be seeing everyone whom he'd grown to know again. Everyone from his roommates to his teachers. Daniel knew that he'd be in for a strange day.

Daniel grabbed his phone from his bedside table and dropped it into his pocket, then paused for a second to wonder if there was anything else which he needed, eventually deciding that he had everything.

Pulling the door open, being careful as to not hit the mirror, Daniel left his bedroom and walked into the living area of his and his roommate's dormitory. Two of the three other people were there, the other two boys, sat on one of the two couches. They were playing a video game which Daniel didn't recognise, one which he probably had never even heard of. It looked obscure as the graphics were slightly wonky even though it was on a fairly recent console, making him wonder if it were poorly made and if his friends were only playing it to make fun of it.

Bryan glanced over his shoulder, probably having heard Daniel approaching. "Morning," he grumbled, sounding slightly unenthusiastic.

"Morning," Daniel replied, questioning the downbeat tone. "You okay?"

"Slept horribly," Bryan stated, having turned his attention back to the TV. Then, once his game character died, he swore under his breath and brushed some of his shoulder-length blonde hair out of his face, probably internally blaming that to be the reason why his character had died.

"As usual," Derek stated, chuckling under his breath. He didn't even look at Daniel or Bryan before he continued. "It's probably because you don't do enough in the day."

"I'm not lazy!" Bryan countered, defensive. He'd turned to look at Derek, his blue eyes piercing into the side of Derek's clean-shaven face. "I just don't sleep well. Insomnia, you know?"

Derek nodded absentmindedly. "I still don't believe that you have insomnia."

"Dude, we've known each other for three years," Bryan stated, looking sick of the conversation. The same few sentences would be traded between the two of them every few weeks, something which Daniel wasn't even certain that they'd realised. "Why don't you believe me?"

Derek rolled his dark brown eyes and returned his full focus to the game, only glancing up when he heard a door open, seeing Claire walking in, fiddling with her long, ginger hair, brushing the left side of her hair behind her left ear, revealing the small, black heart which she'd had tattooed on the left side of her neck the year before as a defiant stance against an ex-boyfriend.

"Are you two arguing *again*?" She let out, sounding both amused and slightly frustrated. She placed her hands on her hips and stared at the two of them from the side, her eyebrows raised as if she were a teacher who'd caught a student on their phone in the middle of a class, her green eyes staring at them, emanating the sarcastic tone which she almost constantly had.

"Of course," Daniel said, leaning over with his arms resting on the top of the back of the couch as he looked between Bryan and Derek, expecting the two of them to have some sort of witty response to Claire.

"He doesn't believe that I have insomnia!" Bryan exclaimed, turning to look at Claire with an expression which perfectly encapsulated how much he couldn't believe it.

"Well, maybe you wouldn't have insomnia if you weren't going at it with Jacob every night," Claire shot back, giving her trademark smirk as she knew that the sentence was enough to shut Bryan up.

Bryan's face flushed red, lighting up like the wick of a candle which had just been touched by a flame. "How do you know?" He spluttered, ignoring the amused looks on Daniel and Derek's faces, Derek's expression excessively smug as he'd just been proved right.

"Our rooms are right next to each other," Claire reminded him. "I can hear you two in the middle of the night."

"Hey, how come we never see him in the mornings?" Daniel questioned, surprised that he hadn't *once* seen Jacob in the morning. He highly doubted that Jacob had the willpower to sneak to Bryan's room, then sneak back to his own every single night or, at least, the majority of nights.

"He doesn't like his roommates to know what he's been up to," Bryan explained. "They're quite childish when it comes to stuff like that because he was caught sneaking back into his room in our first year and said that he'd been out practicing archery," Bryan explained, laughing quietly to himself. "Whenever he gets back late, they always tease him about it."

Derek let out a kind of snorting noise at that, probably making a mental note to use the fact to annoy Bryan, while Daniel and Claire remained silent, processing the information, very slightly amused by it.

It felt strange to be back in university. Daniel was stood around with three of his closest friends, probably three of the closest friends which he'd ever had in his life. He'd just slotted right back into everything as if he'd only been gone for a week on a small holiday. Everything was exactly as he remembered, everything from the constant teasing between Bryan and Derek to the way which Claire stood and looked at them, almost looking slightly disappointed. It felt to Daniel as if he'd returned home.

Daniel walked to the bathroom, used the toilet, washed his hands, brushed his teeth, then walked back out just in time for Derek to remember something.

"Oh, Laura called by before, by the way," Derek said, turning around to look at Daniel. "She said- Christ! You look a mess. Didn't you comb your hair?"

"Yeah, thanks for that," Daniel muttered, grinning a little, knowing that Derek didn't mean the remark. "What did she say?"

"What? Oh, yeah- she said that she wants to see you once you're done with your classes," Derek finished, turning back around to face the TV and continue playing his game.

"Oh, right," Daniel said. "Thanks."

Hearing that Laura wanted to see him just made Daniel feel a very slight tinge of nausea, something which Claire noticed, promptly asking him if he was alright.

"I'm fine," Daniel clarified.

"Really?" Claire asked, sounding critical. "You've gone paler."

Both Derek and Bryan turned around to look at Daniel, the two of them confused, Bryan much more concerned than Derek.

"Oh, yeah! You have," Derek let out. He squinted his eyes slightly as if trying to see if the shift in Daniel's skin tone had come as a result of a trick of his eyes.

"I'm fine," Daniel repeated, chuckling lightly, slightly nervous as he hadn't expected them to notice his feelings. "Just need some water."

Daniel walked to the kitchen sink, grabbed a glass from the draining board, then filled the glass with ice-cold water and drank deeply, finishing the tumbler within moments.

"Anyway, I'd better get to Physics," Daniel said, placing the glass in the sink, struggling with the freezing feeling in his throat as he walked to his room, grabbed his backpack, then rushed to the front door and left, leaving Claire, Bryan and Derek to continue with whatever they were doing.

As Daniel stepped out of the dormitory, he felt a wave of nostalgia upon seeing the hallway. He could remember, mainly out of muscle memory as he'd had to make the trip in the dark, that Laura's dormitory was only a few doors away, five doors to the right of his and across the hall. He even remembered, upon beginning to walk down the hallway and towards the connection which linked the dormitory building to the main campus, that he and Derek had once tested a drone which Claire had created for an engineering assignment and could remember the death-stare which they'd received once she'd found out that they'd nearly lost control of the device and had almost let it tumble down the seven flights of stairs which led from their floor to the ground floor. Daniel could remember just how unimpressed she'd been, but how she'd thanked them later as a few of the scuffs which the device had sustained had revealed to her that one of the propellers was loose to begin with.

Daniel rushed to the stairs after having pulled his phone from his pocket to check the time and, once he realised that he had three minutes to get across the campus and to his class, he simply began sprinting down the hall, leaping down the stairs, nearly twisting his ankle at one point. Daniel silently cursed the fact that he used to get up as late as possible.

It ended up taking Daniel two minutes to sprint across the campus, jumping out of the way of other students and the occasional teacher, the majority of them realising why he was in such a rush, a few of them finding it funny as he rushed by. By the time that Daniel burst into the science building and rushed into his class, he was covered with sweat and both amused and frustrated with himself. Almost everyone else were there already except for a few who were just about to arrive, prompting everyone to look up at him and respond in various ways once they realised what had happened.

"You'd better get to bed earlier, Mister Tale," his professor joked, gesturing towards Daniel's seat with a sideways nod.

Daniel sat down, let out a deep breath as he tried to steady his breathing, then pulled everything which he needed from his bag.

The day went smoothly. Luckily, it was a Wednesday, and, for Daniel, that meant that he only had two lessons: Physics in the morning at half-eight and Biochemistry at eleven, giving him the perfect day to ease back into it.

While leaving Biochemistry, having just walked out of the classroom, heading back to his dormitory to drop his bag off before going to visit Laura to see what she wanted, Daniel realised two things. One: he hadn't remembered at any point throughout the two lessons that he was lucid dreaming. He'd treated the two lessons as he had in real life, paying as close attention as possible, answering as many questions as possible, clarifying everything which he was doing to ensure that he was doing it correctly, and so on. Daniel barely processed that the lessons weren't real, he just slipped back into them so easily. The topics had been ones which he'd practically mastered. His very hasty revision of Biochemistry which he'd done at the end of the last semester of university had allowed him to go over the very basics of the topic and learn it inside out. When it came to Physics, the topic had simply clocked almost straight away. Daniel wondered if the reason why he'd re-experienced those lessons in particular was because he knew the topics and he knew the right answers, but the second thing which he'd realised was that, after straining to remember, those very topics had been presented on that exact date. Daniel had even checked the date to make sure and, as far as he could remember, both of those lessons had been held on that very day when he'd originally gotten through the year, making him wonder if every other lesson which he'd get through if he would choose to stick around would be accurate even if he couldn't remember the topic very well, or even if he didn't understand it in the first place. It was a concept which confused and intrigued him at the same time.

Daniel rushed back up to his dormitory's floor, then back to his dormitory. He pushed the door open and saw that Claire was on the couch, watching a show. She barely acknowledged that he'd walked in.

"Have you seen Laura yet?" She asked, sounding uninterested in what Daniel's answer could have been regardless of the fact that she hadn't even heard his reply yet.

"Not yet," Daniel told her. "I'm just dropping my bag off, then I'll head over there."

"Okay."

Daniel walked into his room, swung his backpack from his shoulder, resting it in front of his cluttered desk, before he turned around and walked back out of the dormitory.

Daniel took a right, walked five doors down, then turned to face Laura's door. He felt as if he needed to psych himself up. He was about to see Laura. She'd probably hug him and kiss him, then explain what she wanted to talk about.

Maybe she's going to break-up with me again, Daniel thought, slightly worried. He hadn't gotten over

Laura. Of course he hadn't. He still loved her, he sort of wanted to still be in a relationship with her, but felt conflicted as he knew that she'd cheated on him. Well, in the future, at least. No, in his reality. In *the* reality. But he was back in university. She hadn't been cheating on him then, had she? She hadn't admitted to doing so, so Daniel hoped not. They were only three years into their six-year relationship. Well...

Daniel rubbed the bridge of his nose, then stretched his fingers out to push against his closed eyes. Trying to make sense of everything was making his head hurt a little. All which he needed to acknowledge was that, as far as he knew, Laura was still innocent. She hadn't done anything to wrong him, so he couldn't reasonably be mad at her. Well, he could be mad at *her*, but not mad at the version of her which he'd be seeing in a few moments.

Daniel let out a frustrated sigh, took a moment to try to calm himself down, then knocked on the door.

Laura pulled it open, smiled, grabbed his arm and pulled him into the room, closing the door quickly before she leaned in and gave him a quick kiss.

"Hey, you," she said, flashing the sweet smile which Daniel had loved- still loved- so dearly. "Want to go out somewhere later?"

Daniel widened his eyes slightly, questioning. "Is that what you called me around for?" He asked, confused. "To ask me on a date?"

Laura giggled a little. "No," she said, walking towards the couch which was almost in the middle of

31

the open-plan area. "I wanted to talk to you about something."

"Something...?" Daniel questioned, urging her to elaborate. "What's the 'something?'"

Laura flopped onto the couch, looking at him while he still stood close to the door, not really wanting to walk into the dormitory and be reminded that the girl in front of him had broken his heart three years later.

"I just want to spend a little more time with you, that's all," she said, tilting her head like a puppy, the little thing which she usually did in hopes of making Daniel find her adorable and agree to what she wanted.

"We already spend a lot of time together," Daniel protested, trying to sound reasonable but, in reality, knowing exactly what he needed to do: get away. Spending more time with Laura had been his downfall. It had been the direct reason as to why he'd ended up failing Biochemistry and not getting his PhD, and trying to fix that had caused him to lose a job which he'd actually quite enjoyed. Agreeing, even though it felt like the right thing to do, was the last thing which Daniel *knew* to do.

"I know," Laura let out, elongating the last word slightly. "I just… I feel like we could spend *more* time together," she said, widening her eyes slightly, the other thing which she tended to do when asking Daniel for something. "Please?"

Daniel let out a breath, trying to make it seem as if he were thinking about a response. He looked up, staring at the ceiling, noticing that there was a long

32

crack which stretched from the wall to his right to just above the door. "Sorry, baby, but I'm a little behind on work."

"Oh," Laura let out, looking down at the ground, looking disappointed. "How far behind?"

"Well, I don't really understand half of what we're doing in Virology right now, and Immunology is definitely getting tougher," Daniel elaborated, making everything up as he went along. In reality, he perfectly understood what was going on in Virology at the time. What was supposed to have been happening in Immunology was one of the subjects which he found the easiest out of the entirety of the rest of the year, too. Daniel just wanted a strong enough reason to be able to convince Laura that he was too busy to ruin his education.

"Oh, I see," Laura muttered, sounding upset. She looked up at Daniel and forced a smile. "It's okay, don't worry."

"I'm not."

Laura rolled her eyes a little. "I can tell you are," she said, standing up, moving towards Daniel. She wrapped her arms around him and rested her head on the inside of his shoulder. "I know that you're feeling guilty that you can't spend more time with me."

"Honestly, I'm not."

Laura looked up at him, a cute smile on her face. "Okay, whatever you say," she said. She gave him a quick kiss, then pulled away. "You'd better get back to work then."

"Yeah," Daniel let out, slightly bitter at the fact that she kept kissing him. He almost felt as if she *knew* that something was wrong and that she was torturing him. Would the event *really* have played out that way had he said "no" in real life? Would she really have been so...

Daniel stepped out of Laura's dormitory and moved back to his own, entering and immediately heading to his room. He flopped onto his bed and let out a long sigh. Visiting Laura had reminded him of something: he'd used to have been afraid of saying "no" to the people closest to him. Had anyone asked him for something or to do something, he would have only been able to decline had the request been something totally unreasonable, hence why he'd given in and had dropped precious revision time to spend more time with Laura. Seeing how Laura had tried to sway him by giving him those looks and by acting all upset felt unreasonable when, in reality, Daniel was almost certain that she hadn't been fazed. Otherwise, what would she have expected? They were in their last year of university. Of course they were going to be busy! How could she expect him to just push everything to one side for her? She couldn't have possibly expected him to agree and waste valuable time with her, right?

Daniel rolled onto his back and stared at the ceiling. He was going to stay in university. He'd made up his mind. He was going to stay, and he was going to change things. He was going to live the life which he *really* wanted. He was going to make sure that he'd get all of the grades which he needed. He was going to quit his job when it was time to quit instead of being fired. He was going to force himself to be much more honest and do what *he* wanted instead of what everyone else wanted from him. He was going to change himself for the better. Daniel made the promise to do so to himself.

Chapter 3

A few days passed. They passed way too quickly in Daniel's eyes, especially given that he had a slight fear of just waking up and leaving everything behind again. Every time when he'd wake up, he'd bolt upright and stare at the room around him, making sure that he hadn't woken up in the real world. As soon as he'd realise that he was still in university, he'd take a few deep breaths and promptly, within five minutes, forget about the ordeal.

As he had on his first day back in university, Daniel had slipped into routine and had completely forgotten that he was dreaming while in lessons though, occasionally, that would also spill into the rest of his dreaming life. Once, the day before, he'd been sat on the couch with Derek, the two of them trying to beat a level in a game which they'd found excessively hard, when Daniel remembered a trick which he'd learned for that specific game. He'd learned the trick a year later when visiting Derek who'd promptly told him about it, and, upon realising as such, Daniel froze and realised just how scary it was to lose a grip on reality. Derek had asked him what was wrong, and Daniel had simply brushed it off as if he'd been shocked that he hadn't thought of the trick before. He told Derek, Derek mastered it, and they moved on.

Something else which Daniel had noticed was that Laura had been acting a little off with him whenever they'd meet up to spend a small amount of time together. He'd chalked it up to the fact that he hadn't given her what she'd wanted, but doubted that she'd be so unreasonable. Daniel, for obvious reasons, didn't want to spend a lot of time with her, but he just couldn't bring himself to cut her out of his life or to break-up with her. It seemed incredibly strange to Daniel whenever he considered it, but he knew that he was genuinely holding onto each time when they'd meet up for as little as ten minutes as if he knew that he wouldn't ever see her again within a few days. He was thinking of their brief interactions as much more than what they really were. Every time he'd bid farewell to Laura, he'd almost feel warm inside until he'd remember what had happened in reality, promptly trying to push the feelings away. Laura, in his dream, at least, hadn't done anything against him. She hadn't wronged him in any way. She was the same Laura from when Daniel had been in his last year of university. Why should he treat her as if she'd broken his heart in the dream, too? It was strange, but Daniel didn't feel as if she deserved the treatment. If anything, Daniel wanted to distance himself from her to stop himself from having to feel pained upon every meeting and departure, but he also wanted to spend a lot of time with her because she was the innocent Laura whom he'd fallen in love with, not the monster who'd hurt him.

Daniel thought that it would be a good idea to check on her and try to find out what was wrong.

Daniel sat in his bed, having just woken up, and yawned. He still found it strange that he could feel tired while asleep and, what was even weirder, was that he could dream in his dream. He could very vaguely remember that he'd dreamt that he and Claire had been riding on the back of camels in Egypt, brandishing swords and armour, riding towards a battle which they just couldn't find no matter how hard they tried.

After forcing himself out from underneath the duvet, Daniel hopped to the ground and pulled his clothes on; clothes which he'd worn the day before after having realised that he'd worn more or less the same thing for a few days straight. Daniel pulled the blue jeans, the black t-shirt, the white hoodie, the black socks and, then, his unbranded black trainers on. He checked himself out in the mirror, making sure that he looked presentable, then stepped out to greet Bryan who was the only one awake.

After having had to rush across the campus to get to Biochemistry on his first day back, Daniel had decided to get up earlier, now climbing out of bed an hour and a half before his first lesson of most days. The only exception was Friday, where his first lesson was at eleven, and Daniel didn't think that sleeping until half-nine was healthy.

"Morning," Bryan let out, then yawned.

"Morning," Daniel replied, resisting the urge to copy the yawn. "You know, if you're so tired, you don't have to get up an hour before your lessons."

Bryan glanced at him, looking away from the book which he was reading for only two seconds. "I can't get up any later," he replied, turning back to his book. "Too risky. I hit snooze at least three times every morning already."

Daniel snickered. "Then, maybe hold off on your meetings with Jacob," he suggested before jumping over the back of the couch and landing in the empty space next to Bryan, making him jump when the thud sounded, having scared him slightly.

Bryan looked slightly flustered. "Can't do that, either," he muttered, almost too quietly for Daniel to hear.

Daniel ignored Bryan's response, knowing that, no matter what he could possibly say, Bryan wouldn't alter anything to be less tired. It was almost as if he *wanted* to be tired. It was almost as if he liked having the excuse at hand, probably in case he'd mess something simple up as it would be a good excuse to keep Derek's banter at bay.

Daniel let out a light sigh, then stood up after a few moments despite having just sat down, heading for the bathroom to brush his teeth and to have a quick shower. He wasn't entirely sure about what he even wanted to do to pass the time. Given that, every day, he and his roommates had their alarms set for different times, he couldn't ever plan an event. He couldn't rely on Derek, Bryan or Claire to be up at the same time as him and willing to do something with him to pass the time. It was a problem which Daniel didn't know how to solve without simply giving in and sleeping for longer.

Daniel showered quickly then brushed his teeth. He walked out of the bathroom while adjusting his t-shirt after having just returned it to his body, and was greeted by Derek almost walking into him as he came out of his room, having woken up only a few moments before.

"Morning," Derek grunted, moving around Daniel to go into the bathroom.

Bryan looked over his shoulder, having put his book down for a moment to do so. "What's up with him?" He questioned with an eyebrow raised.

The bathroom door closed, no response coming from Derek as he either didn't hear the question or didn't care to chime in with an answer.

Daniel shrugged. "Might be a bad day of lessons," he suggested, unsure and unwilling to spend time contemplating an answer which Derek could provide on his own.

It took another ten minutes for Claire to get up, her tall, almost elegant physique contrasting the grouchy expression which she had on her face after having just woken up, a large fraction of her hair jutting out in different directions as if she were cosplaying a studded bracelet.

"Sleep well, Sleeping Beauty?" Derek taunted, having come out of the bathroom a minute or so before after showering.

Claire gave him an extremely sarcastic smile, then walked to the bathroom.

Daniel spent the remainder of his time that morning playing a game with Derek while Bryan read close-by and while Claire crammed some revision notes which she'd taken the night before as she'd been told that she had a mini-exam to do within a week to show how she was coping with the work. By the time that Daniel realised that he had to leave for Immunology in order to get there on time, no-one had moved an inch except for Derek who was periodically checking the time, trying not to let himself slip into a trance and end up late for his lesson.

Daniel had three lessons and breezed through them, still without acknowledging that he was asleep. It was only when he came out of Virology that he remembered that it would be a good idea to talk with Laura just to make sure that she was okay when he remembered what had happened in reality, something which had gotten him down a little.

After dropping his backpack off in his dormitory, Daniel was just about to head to Laura's dormitory when Claire pulled him aside, wanting to ask for a favour.

"Could you make sure that neither Bryan nor Derek steal these?" She asked, holding up a bag of sweets which, Daniel knew, were Claire's favourite.

"Yeah, sure," Daniel replied, surprised that Claire had to ask him to keep an eye out. Though, he did also know that Derek and Bryan considered all of the food in the dormitory to belong to the four of them yet, as Daniel had caught Derek doing once, they liked to hide their favourite snacks from the others.

"Thanks," Claire said. "Last time I got some, Bryan stole them within the same day," she recalled looking annoyed.

Daniel quickly exhaled from his nose, slightly amused but also identifying with the annoyance as Bryan had also stolen snacks from him before.

"Just hide them well," Daniel instructed as he left the room, closing the door behind him.

The interaction was enough to distract Daniel from fully comprehending that he was about to see Laura, something which was fortunate as, upon approaching her door, he felt a wave of worry. Why had she been off with him? Had he done something wrong? Daniel didn't want to end up being shouted at and, weirdly, he didn't want to have to feel guilty about something when Laura had *definitely* done much worse to him.

Daniel knocked on the door, using his left hand to rub his face slightly as if he were trying to rub the sudden stress out of his mind.

After a moment of waiting, the door opened, and Daniel was greeted by Jason Dunn, a friend of Derek's and one of Laura's roommates. Jason was older than a lot of other people in the university, somewhere in his thirties, having already had a small career, having already gotten married, having already had a child. According to Derek, Jason had fancied a career change, deciding to study to become a detective, and had only moved into the dormitories as it was much cheaper than travelling from his and his family's apartment every day. He was somehow managing to balance some light work, having a family, *and* having a full-time education. A lot of people in the university were in awe of the man.

"Alright, Daniel?" Jason asked, in the middle of eating a chocolate bar. "Here to see Laura?"

Daniel nodded, nervous. Jason was making it sound as if Laura had called him there for an interrogation.

Jason let Daniel walk into the room, where he saw Reece sat on a couch, looking at him quizzically alongside Sabrina, the two of them looking extremely confused to see Daniel.

"I thought you were in there…" Sabrina began, looking from Daniel to the door to Laura's room, then back at Daniel. Her face dropped and she jumped up from the couch, storming towards Laura's room.

Daniel stood there, confused, wondering what was going on. Why was Sabrina angry? Surely she hadn't seen something…

Sabrina flung the door open and, there, on Laura's bed, was Laura and another boy whom Daniel vaguely recognised, having seen him on campus, wrapped around each other, clearly having just been kissing quite intimately.

Daniel's heart dropped alongside his facial expression. Again? *Again*? But, she'd been faithful at this time, right? She hadn't admitted to cheating on him in university... Had she *really* done that in real life? *No,* Daniel told himself. *I'm dreaming. How would I know of something like this without having been told?*

But that didn't stop Daniel from being angry. It might have been his subconscious which had forced Laura to cheat on him again, but seeing it just made him furious.

Daniel turned and simply began walking to the door while Sabrina screamed at the boy to get out, then began screaming at Laura.

The sound of footsteps came quickly from behind Daniel, the boy rushing past him and pulling the door open, quickly zooming out of it as if he was being chased by a pack of lions. Then, after the boy had left, Daniel felt a desperate arm grab around his shoulders, trying to pull him back.

"I'm sorry!" Laura cried, probably crying due to the sound of her voice.

Daniel stopped in his tracks, then spun around so violently that he forced Laura's arm off of him, making it slam into the wall beside them.

"You're only sorry that you were caught," he stated, his voice cold but with the heat of fury clearly underlining his words.

Laura gave him a pleading look, then turned to look at Jason, Reece and Sabrina, the three of them staring at her with cold eyes, their stances showing just how much they were scolding her. Sabrina had her hands on her hips, looking stern. Jason had his arms crossed, looking extremely intimidating, especially because he was older than everyone else in the room. Reece simply looked disappointed, genuinely struggling to look at Laura, looking more at Daniel, showing as much sympathy as he could through his second-hand anger and surprise.

"Listen," Laura began. "I-"

"No, *you* listen," Daniel interrupted, able to feel the anger beginning to seep into his already spiteful words, though he made a conscious effort to keep his voice at a reasonable level. "You somehow expect me to spend *more* time with you instead of doing work that's more important than this relationship clearly was to you, and when I say no, you strop and act like the child which you are."

Laura looked shocked and hurt, but Daniel wasn't done.

"You're always wanting me to do things for you, you're always expecting me to give you more time than you deserve, you're always manipulating me into giving you what you want, and you've never *once* considered what type of effect that has on me!" He exclaimed, realising that his voice was getting louder and louder as he let everything out. He tried to calm himself down slightly, but immediately found that he couldn't. Because he'd started, there wasn't a chance that he'd be able to stop or to tone it down before finishing his rant. "*I've* always been the one holding this together by giving you whatever you've asked for, which is clear because as soon as I said 'no,' you pranced off to someone else to get your needs!" Daniel pointed a finger at her and gestured in a random direction as he spoke, nearly hitting her in the face with his hand, though he wouldn't have been bothered had the hit connected. "After everything which I've done for you, you repay me by cheating on me!"

Laura tried to interject but failed.

"I don't want to hear any excuses!" Daniel shouted. "For once in your life, admit that you're *wrong*!"

Everyone was quiet for a moment. Laura didn't speak, and so Daniel stormed off after muttering that the relationship was over, very deeply satisfied with himself.

Chapter 4

Daniel went to bed feeling a mixture of sadness and satisfaction. Daniel woke up to feel a mixture of contentment and hatred. What had happened the previous day with Laura had been exceptionally strange. Daniel knew that his subconscious was to blame. He was having a bad dream where his girlfriend had cheated on him. The only difference was that she'd cheated on him in reality, too, making Daniel wonder if his mind just couldn't accept the idea of acting as if she never had just because Daniel was experiencing a time where she *shouldn't* have. Therefore, Daniel concluded, Laura was practically destined to cheat on him at *some* point within his lucid dream regardless. Still, though, that didn't affect how it made Daniel feel, whether immediately upon opening his eyes in the morning or upon beginning his day and noticing each of his emotions.

After climbing out of bed, probably too nonchalant than he should have realistically been given that he'd actually *witnessed* being cheated on the night before, Daniel silenced his alarm, grabbed some clean clothes from the miscoloured chest of drawers, and got dressed, climbing into some grey jeans, a white t-shirt, blue socks and the unbranded, black trainers which he wore every day. Afterwards, he stepped out of his room and was greeted by Derek, Bryan and Claire already up, something which he'd been anticipating as it was a Tuesday, the four of them with an early class that day.

"Alright, mate?" Derek asked, turning around from watching Claire as she played a game on the TV.

"Yeah," Daniel replied, stopping in his tracks. He realised that the three of them would probably end up being softer with him given what had happened. Once Daniel had returned to the dormitory, Claire had been extremely confused as he'd only left a few minutes before, and asked what was wrong, having heard distant shouts but having not put the puzzle pieces together. Once Daniel had explained what had happened, he'd had to restrain her from rushing over to Laura's dormitory and, to quote her, "kicking her scummy face into the back of her skull."

Naturally, once Bryan and Derek had returned from their lessons, Claire had recounted what Daniel had told her and, again, naturally, the two of them had become livid at the news, though neither of them had decided to storm over there. Derek had done his best to comfort Daniel who, at the time, *was* feeling upset after having seen Laura with another man, while Bryan had called a few of their other friends around for the group of nine to have a night together to distract Daniel from the ordeal. Daniel appreciated what his friends had done to help him.

Derek gave a light nod. "Claire's-"

"If you say I'm terrible at this," Claire cut

across, trying her best to sound genuinely threatening without intending to do anything.

"Okay, she's amazing at this game," Derek stated, sounding extremely sarcastic. He turned back to the TV to focus on Claire's gameplay as she promptly fumbled the controls and sent her character falling off of a cliff and to its demise.

"The bathroom's free if you want to shower," Bryan informed Daniel, looking up from his book for a moment to flash a quick smile towards Daniel.

"Oh, right," Daniel let out, having forgotten that he'd intended to freshen-up before leaving for Biochemistry. "Thanks."

Daniel walked into the bathroom and, after closing the door, let out a long sigh. He was in a strange type of purgatory where he was destined to haphazardly switch between feeling nonchalant, albeit slightly discomforted, to feeling a horrible and probably dangerous mixture of sadness and anger. One minute, he'd feel somewhat normal, maybe slightly satisfied as Laura had been caught and definitely shamed by her roommates but, the next minute, he'd just feel upset for having had to see her cheating on him in the first place. It was draining. No matter what the positives were, the negatives would constantly peek into his mind and remind him of the unpleasant emotions which came with the ordeal.

After ten minutes, Daniel walked out of the bathroom. He'd showered and brushed his teeth and was ready to start the day properly but, upon walking back into the main living area, Derek had some news for Daniel.

"Everyone's heard, by the way," he informed Daniel, confusing him for a moment as he wasn't sure what Derek was referring to.

"Heard what?" Daniel inquired, pulling his phone out of his pocket to check the time before sliding it back into the pocket. He had fifty minutes before he had to leave, and there must have only been a handful of minutes before Derek and Bryan had to leave, too. Claire had already disappeared for her first lesson.

"Laura," Derek said, looking slightly uncomfortable as he said the name, maybe worrying that just hearing Laura's name would upset Daniel.

"Everyone's heard?" Daniel repeated, not very affected by the sound of Laura's name. "How?" He moved to the couch and sat on the arm of it even though there was an empty space next to the arm.

"Well, it might have been Henry's fault," Derek admitted. "When he came around last night, he wasn't very happy to hear about what happened."

"Yeah?" Daniel urged. "And?"

"Well, you know how he sort of struggles to keep big things to himself?" Derek asked rhetorically, scratching his eyebrow as he spoke. "I think he sort of… ranted to other people over text about it, and it *might* have spread everywhere."

Daniel shrugged, not caring too much. "And?" He asked.

Derek gave him a blank look. "Well, there's

nothing else, really," he finished, taken aback. "Does it bother you?"

"Well, not really," Daniel admitted, turning to look at the carpeted floor. "No-one's going to blame me for breaking up with her. If anything, *she'll* be treated differently, and I'm fine with that," he explained, feeling slightly guilty for acknowledging that he wouldn't even care if Laura ended up losing all of her respect and her friends. She'd hurt him twice. Badly. She probably deserved it, at least to some extent.

Derek tilted his head slightly, considering Daniel's words. "Fair enough," he let out after a moment, slightly bemused. He glanced at his watch. "I have to go," he said, standing up and tapping Bryan on the arm as he did so, snatching Bryan's attention from his book, telling him that it was time to leave.

Bryan and Derek headed to their rooms, grabbed their bags, then left the dormitory after calling goodbyes to Daniel, leaving him alone for what would be around fifty minutes before it would be time to head for his lesson.

Daniel sighed, staring at the blank TV. He wondered what the day would be like. If practically everyone had heard about what had happened himself and Laura, would people be treating him differently? Would people be much more sympathetic or empathic towards him? Would people go out of their way to be kind to him? Would people try to stay away from him out of fear of being forced to comfort him if he'd start crying? Daniel, being honest with himself, wasn't sure if he'd be comfortable with everyone being so... weird. He didn't *want* people to treat him differently. Yes, Laura had practically gauged his heart out at this point, but did everyone else have to deal with comforting him in regards to his problem when he was almost completely fine? Of course not! Usually, Daniel would have welcomed the toned-up kindness with open arms, but he didn't *need* the kindness.

For a moment, Daniel almost felt scared. He almost felt as if he were preparing to take part in a massive public-speaking campaign, one which was being broadcasted all over the world for everyone to see and judge and laugh at if he'd mess up. Daniel genuinely felt nervous just because he'd be going to Biochemistry and he didn't know how people would treat him. It seemed silly to worry about it. It seemed much more stupid than worrying about moving to a new school in the middle of the school year, something which Daniel had never experienced, but something which he'd heard a lot about and classed as completely ridiculous. What was the point in worrying? If people would be kind to him, what was the need to feel scared? Where had the fear even come from?

Daniel sighed, leaned back into the couch, then closed his eyes. *Shut up*, he told his brain, trying to quell the train- no, the cruise ship- no, the fleet of thoughts from bothering him any more. It was just a lesson. He only had to deal with Biochemistry, then he'd know what to expect for the next day, then maybe the day after before people would start drifting towards treating him normally again.

Daniel spent forty-five minutes watching a show which he was struggling to get into until he realised that it was time to go and, with one last pang of nervousness, he grabbed his backpack and left the dormitory.

As Daniel walked towards the stairs, he passed a few people who were either on their way back from their rooms or on their way to lessons. Daniel didn't notice many of them as they didn't notice him, but as he neared the stairs, Daniel caught sight of a boy whom he didn't know at all giving him a slightly solemn look, then a light nod to acknowledge Daniel.

Daniel returned the small nod, then kept his head down while going down the stairs. Not everyone whom he came across would give him a look which explicitly said "sorry about that thing," but when he'd notice someone who did, Daniel flashed a small, meek smile and simply continued walking.

Okay, he thought. *So far, it's not too bad.*

Daniel wasn't sure whether or not the people around him would progress from knowing looks to actually talking to him, but he expected that, if it *was* going to happen, it would be within his lessons. The realisation made him feel weird. He didn't necessarily feel nervous anymore, just a slight tinge of awkwardness. He didn't want to be the centre of attention, especially given that he hadn't done something to deserve it. Daniel almost felt slightly suffocated with the knowledge that people would escalate their treatment of him, at least, probably, but it wasn't as bad as Daniel had anticipated given that he was already experiencing a fraction of it.

It took a few minutes for Daniel to reach his Biochemistry class and, once he entered, he was happy to see that no-one seemed to notice him arriving. Well, no-one except for his professor.

"Daniel," his professor muttered, motioning for Daniel for approach him. "Are you okay?"

Daniel let out a small, barely noticeable breath. "I'm fine, sir."

"Are you sure? I've had the same happen to me, so I know how bad it feels."

"Really, sir, I'm fine," Daniel insisted, trying to add a lace of finality to his tone without sounding hot-headed and disrespectful of the fact that his teacher was checking on him.

The man nodded lightly. "Okay," he said. "But don't worry too much about this lesson. If you need to leave any point, just give me a shout and I'll email you the work, a few examples and an explanation, okay?"

Daniel nodded slightly, thankful that he was being offered what many students in the class would have probably considered a luxury given that it was early in the morning.

Daniel walked away from his professor, heading to his seat. A few people had noticed him, something which Daniel acknowledged with a few, small, awkward smiles in their direction as they gave him what Daniel could have only described as eyes which tried to be empathetic.

As soon as Daniel sat down, he pulled everything which he needed from his bag and laid it on the table in front of him, then went to close his bag and realised that someone was stood next to him.

"Um, hi," the girl said, bending over a little so that her face was in Daniel's line of vision even though she wasn't towering over him too much while standing, probably only around average height. She had long, black, wavy hair and blue eyes which stood out to Daniel though confused him as he couldn't see any intent in them which would explain whether she was going to make a passing comment or a lengthened, empathetic statement. He couldn't tell, even from looking at the rest of her round, lightly freckled face what she intended to do. She looked entirely nonchalant, if not slightly embarrassed. "You don't know me, but-"

"You've heard about what's happened," Daniel finished for her, seeing her nod very slightly, almost looking embarrassed.

"Yeah," she confirmed, crouching down in front of Daniel's table. "So… well, if you need someone to talk to, you can talk to me."

Daniel looked at her, stunned.

"I've been through the same thing before, so if you need any advice," the girl added quickly, looking extremely uncomfortable. She slid a strip of paper towards Daniel with a number on it. "That's my phone number," she explained, then gave a quick smile. "Phone me or text me whenever you like."

And, with that, the girl walked away, leaving

55

Daniel to sit there, extremely taken aback. He watched the girl return to her seat, expecting her to turn to her friends and laugh about it, but she sat alone, not talking to anyone. For a moment, Daniel had wondered if the moment had been a prank or something, but he shrugged it off and took a moment to input the number into his phone, not knowing what else to do to pass the time. There was still a minute before the lesson would start, so Daniel guessed that it would be a good pass-time.

After inputting the number into his phone, Daniel sent a quick text, simply asking for the girl's name.

Across the room, the girl pulled her phone out, replied to the text, then turned around to look at Daniel and flashed a smile. Maybe she hadn't been expecting Daniel to actually *want* to talk to her.

Elisha. That was the girl's name, Daniel realised upon reading the text.

Thanks for this, he typed, then sent it.

Daniel slid his phone back into his pocket as the professor decided to begin the lesson, Elisha doing the same across the room.

Chapter 5

Meeting Elisha ended up being much more beneficial to Daniel than he'd initially expected. Directly after getting done with the day's lessons, he'd sent her a text, wanting to get to know her better as he wouldn't feel extremely comfortable opening up to someone whom he didn't know.

The two of them shared an initial conversation directly after their school day had ended, getting to know each other as best as possible. Daniel, of course, couldn't convey that he was technically from the future, making it very slightly stressful as he typed everything out, reading over each text a number of times just to make sure that he hadn't let anything slip which didn't add up, though, after a while, he began to calm down slightly, especially when it came to learning more about Elisha.

Elisha, like Daniel, was interested in doing *something* with science. Unlike Daniel who simply wanted to be somewhere within the field, Elisha wanted to specifically work as a biologist, having had to take the same course as Daniel to do so. Daniel hadn't even previously realised that she was in all of his classes, sat very far away from him most of the time, but there, nonetheless. He'd only realised as, once he'd left

Biochemistry, he saw that, ahead of him, Elisha was walking in the same direction and, after some time, he saw that she was going to his Immunology class. Aside from her studies, Elisha shared that she largely spent her time studying, that she didn't think that she had enough time to balance a social life, an education *and* part-time work, so she settled for over-studying to ease the stress and the guilt which would inevitably come with taking a few hours off to spend with her friends. Largely, the rest of the information presented to Daniel was miscellaneous, not a lot to do with hobbies as she didn't have much time to partake in activities, and so she didn't bother mentioning any, leaving only things as trivial as her birthday or her religious stance: atheist, similar to Daniel's agnosticism.

After having gotten to know each other initially, the two of them spent some time apart, Elisha so she could study while Daniel simply needed to finish a few pieces of homework, though, later on, they continued their conversation, this time moving to the problem at hand. Even though Daniel was, as he viewed it, largely over what had happened with Laura as he'd already had the few days before to accept that she'd cheated on him in the real world, Daniel discovered that still felt upset about it, nonetheless. He didn't know where the emotion had come from, but he could only theorise with himself that he wasn't entirely over everything which had happened in the real world. He'd been dating Laura for six years. For her to just turn around and unload such hurtful information so suddenly hadn't been pleasant, to say the least. Daniel tried his best to convey the feelings to Elisha without giving away what had really happened, not wanting to confuse things by mentioning to her that he was asleep. Even though Daniel doubted that he'd be able to explain exactly how he was feeling to her, he somehow managed it and was dragged into a discussion with her in regards to how he'd be able to distract himself from the ordeal.

The discussion, contrasting Daniel's original expectations, helped largely. He didn't realise that he had any lasting feelings directly linked to Laura herself other than the hope that she'd have some form of punishment suitable for what she'd done to him, something which he felt had already largely arrived as she, alongside the boy whom she'd cheated on Daniel with, were practically being segregated by the rest of the university's population. Aside from that hope, Daniel found that he still had some lingering sadness, something which he played off to Elisha as sadness stemming from the sudden end of a three-year-long relationship, but which he knew stemmed from the reminder of what had ended the six-year-long relationship.

Something which Daniel ended up realising and fully comprehending while they talked was the fact that he, even though what had happened in reality had happened, didn't have the strength to end things with Laura without a good motive. He simply still loved her and, as he'd noticed before, craved her company and her attention even though he knew what she'd done to him and even though he could still feel the lingering, stabbing pain which came with the thought of her having not loved him for so long. The realisation was something which, in a weird way, almost made Daniel want to thank Laura for cheating on him with that guy. It gave him the power which he'd needed to do what he'd needed to do on the first day back.

The two of them, after having discussed Daniel's problem, decided that they were getting along fairly well and, as a result, they weren't opposed to spending time together as friends, not as a mock-therapist and client. Neither of them knew when they'd spend time together, neither of them knew what they'd do to have fun while spending time together, but they both agreed that they weren't opposed to the concept, something which Daniel was happy about as he genuinely liked Elisha and thought of her as a sweet girl who'd gone out of her way just to try to help him, something which she'd succeeded in doing. He definitely wasn't against having a friend like that.

Daniel walked into his room after having just finished a lesson and sat down at his desk, looking at the Curriculum Vitae in front of him. He'd already filled it out and was looking for places online where he could send it, wanting to get a job as, seeing as he'd already lived through and understood the lessons which he was taking, didn't feel very stressed and was, to put it simply, bored. Daniel guessed that getting a job as he had his first time around would be beneficial, especially given that spare money wouldn't do him any harm, and he didn't have the heart to materialise it in front of him. Besides, the last time when he'd worked a part-time job in his last year of university, Daniel had largely spent the money on Laura. In fact, he'd only applied for jobs because he and Laura were spending so much time together and he wanted to treat her to "luxurious" dinners or to a film every now and then. Plus, at the time, Daniel wasn't struggling when it came to time. He was spending so much time with Laura and avoiding studying that a few extra hours a week spent working in that restaurant wouldn't affect much. Laura hadn't complained, probably because he'd shared his desire to work to spoil her, so he'd sent out applications and had found the job which, honestly, Daniel wouldn't have minded falling back on when he'd failed to earn his PhD. The only problem was that, in trying to save his PhD, Daniel had slacked off work for a few weeks to cram more and more notes and had, after a month of not showing up or of showing up late, been fired.

As Daniel scrolled through the listings for places which were hiring, Daniel had the idea to have a look at the restaurant which he'd previously worked in. Would it hurt to go back and retry the miniature career? Probably not. He was looking for a job, anyway, and he really *did* like working there, so...

After a minute of searching, Daniel came across the restaurant. They were hiring, he noticed, so he grabbed his CV and rushed to the library to photocopy the document. Daniel knew that, even though he could probably apply online, it would make him look better if he'd deliver the document in person. He'd done so last time, having thought of the trick, and had gotten the job. Daniel didn't know if that had been the reason why he'd edged someone else out or not, but he wasn't going to take the chance of possibly losing the listing. He wanted his old job back, mainly for nostalgia reasons.

After a few minutes of walking, Daniel found the library and promptly headed to the photocopier. He stuck the CV under the lid, pressed the buttons to make the magic work, then waited for a moment while the document printed. Once it had finished, he grabbed it and returned to his dormitory, dropping off the original copy just in case before quickly telling Claire, Bryan and Derek where he was going.

"Good luck!" Bryan called after him, Daniel barely catching the words before he pulled the door closed behind him.

Daniel made his way down the stairs and onto the campus, then found his way into the city. He could still remember the route to the restaurant as he'd probably taken it at least fifty times before he'd began slacking off. All he had to do was take a left after leaving the campus, then the first right available, the third left, past three turnings on the left and then…

Daniel let out a breath as he stopped in front of the restaurant, looking up to stare at the sign.

"Okay," he muttered to himself under his breath, then unconsciously ran his left hand through his hair, trying to neaten it up at least somewhat. He knew that he was only going to be requesting to see the manager to give them the copy of his CV, but Daniel guessed that, if he looked tidy, he'd be perceived as reliable.

Daniel walked into the restaurant, then spent a minute walking around, looking for the manager whom he didn't know.

Daniel knew, given the time, that the current manager was close to leaving the job. He didn't know how long they were staying, but knew that the manager whom he'd known and had worked for, Dale, was being trained by them and was due to take over fairly soon. Daniel had been hired only a week-or-so after the new manager had taken over, possibly giving himself an extra chance as Dale didn't have much experience when it came to hiring people. Maybe he'd seen something which he'd liked about Daniel and only focused on that instead of looking at the bigger picture, something which, upon considering the possibility, made Daniel feel slightly nervous about handing his CV in to the prior manager.

Once Daniel spotted the manager, he approached just as the woman was walking into the kitchen, probably heading to check something.

"Excuse me," Daniel said, catching her attention. She turned around and, contrasting Daniel's fears of looking and sounding extremely stern, tilted her head and smiled sweetly at him.

"What's up?" She asked, looking genuinely interested.

The woman was fairly short, her eyes level with the CV as Daniel held it up to his chest to show her.

"You have a job listing online," Daniel said, feeling the relief flush over him at the fact that the manager wasn't an evil witch who'd shoot him down within moments. "For a new waiter. Are you still accepting applications?"

The woman nodded, somewhat eagerly. "Yeah!" She let out, enthusiastic, taking the CV from Daniel's hands. She smiled at him again. "Leave this with me. I'll have a look over it and, if you're of interest, I'll call you for an interview, okay?"

Daniel nodded lightly, flashing a small smile alongside a relieved breath. "Thanks," he said.

"You should hear from me within a few days," the woman told him, then, after somehow politely stating that the conversation was over with only her body language, turned and walked into the kitchen, the CV clutched tightly in her right hand as if she was scared of dropping it.

Daniel turned, too, walking out of the restaurant. Again, after standing before it, he looked up at the sign. "So far, so good," he whispered to himself as he began to head back in the direction of the university.

After getting back to the university, Daniel noticed that a few people would look at him when he would pass, but definitely not as many people as the previous few days. A handful of days had passed since he'd caught Laura cheating on him and, as he'd initially expected, everyone's interest and concern regarding the topic was beginning to fade away. Daniel hardly ever noticed anyone giving him sympathetic looks. The only person who'd consistently check in on how he was feeling was Elisha. Bryan, Derek and Claire would ask occasionally but, as they'd admitted once, they didn't want to bring it up too often out of fear of striking a nerve and upsetting Daniel, something which he understood. Elisha, however, would text him at least once a day asking about how he felt, asking if he was getting over it or not. One thing which hadn't changed, however, was how people were treating Laura. Daniel hadn't seen anything himself, but Bryan and Laura shared a class and, according to Bryan, no-one was talking to her except for when it was necessary. The professor, for obvious reasons, couldn't shut her out, so she'd be communicating with Laura regularly, but no-one else would if they could avoid it. It was almost as if Laura was a virus and talking to her would be opening the lungs and inviting the virus inside of the body.

Daniel entered the dormitory and was immediately rounded-up on by his roommates.

"How did it go?" Derek asked, kneeling on the seat portion of the couch, leaning his arms on the back of it. "Did you get interviewed?"

"No," Daniel responded simply. "They're going to have a look at my CV and see if they want me there."

Claire made a slightly bitter look, something which Bryan noticed.

"What's that look for?" He asked, intrigued, snatching the attention of Derek and Daniel, the two of them looking at Claire, wondering what look Bryan was referring to.

"Well, I'd have thought that they'd look over the CV immediately and ask a few questions," she admitted, shrugging lightly. "I'm not saying that you won't get the job!" She backtracked, holding her hands up to Daniel as if to show that she wasn't going to hurt him. "It's just not really a good sign."

"I got the job last time," Daniel stated, then froze when he realised what he'd said. Neither Bryan nor Claire noticed anything wrong with the sentence, but Derek did. He looked at Daniel, an eyebrow raised.

"You've worked there before?"

"No!" Daniel let out, scared that openly admitting what was going on would somehow wake himself up or, at the very least, drastically alter how his roommates would interact with him. "I mean- the last time I got a job."

Bryan and Claire were looking at Daniel, trying to figure out what was wrong with the previous sentence, maybe slightly intrigued by the impression which Derek had gotten.

They were all silent for a moment, then Derek shrugged it off. "I guess that means that it won't *definitely* be bad, then," he stated, glancing at Claire to see if she had any objections to that idea, to which she had none.

Daniel let out a small sigh, having scared himself. Although, the moment had raised a question: what *would* happen if he told someone that he knew that he was asleep? Would it have any effect? If he were in control of the dream, would he be able to just flip things back to normal? Act like it never happened? Or was the lucid dream a set timeline, like an actual life. If he'd say something or do something, would it drastically affect things in the future? Could he defy physics if he really wanted to? Could he simply imagine being at graduation, having passed his exams, and then *be* there, *experience* it? If Daniel could, he didn't want to. It wouldn't feel as if he'd earned it, more as if he'd asked a genie for an experience. There wouldn't be any emotion behind the memory which it would form. When he'd wake up, he'd want to be able to think: "yes, I did that. Maybe it wasn't real, but I *did* it." Daniel wanted more than anything for the events which he was experiencing to *feel* authentic. He wanted to go to bed and worry about finishing a piece of homework on time or tire himself out by studying. Why? Well, university was probably the best time in Daniel's life. Sure, he'd failed to get his PhD, but he'd had fun. He'd dated a girl whom he still felt to be at least somewhat precious to him, he'd met friends who, after university, he still kept in touch with regularly, and he'd definitely had a few vital life-experiences. There were negatives, of course. He'd felt crushed when he hadn't passed his Biochemistry exam and couldn't qualify for his PhD. He'd felt flattened when his part-time job which he'd loved had been ripped away from him. He'd been incredibly angry with himself when he'd turned down an opportunity to see a childhood for the first time in years only for the man to die from a freak accident the day directly after they would have met up. All of the positives and the negatives combined made Daniel think of his university years as a balanced life. Too much positivity would have made him weaker. Too much negativity would have beaten him down until he wouldn't have had any more drive in him, any more confidence, any more motivation. He'd had a healthy dose of the two. An extended knowledge and a failed PhD in Biochemistry. Long lasting friendships and the loss of someone whom he deemed as one of the closest friends whom he'd ever had. Spending what must have been hours simply laughing about random things, having fun and lashing out at the people closest to him as a result of losing a long-time friend. A very valuable employment experience and the loss of a part-time job which he'd loved. A partner whom he'd cherished and a weakness when it came to saying "no" to people. Incredibly fun parties which he'd spent bonding with his friends, simply letting himself go, and a smoking addiction which he just couldn't drop as soon as he'd been introduced to cigarettes.

Daniel tried to push the thoughts away. It was too deep for him to want to think about. Why worry about messing something up? It could *raise* the chances of him messing something up if he was to keep thinking about it. Daniel had been gradually acknowledging that he was asleep less and less. It was better that way. He'd think about things which had happened in the real world as if he'd talked to a psychic and had been told what would happen, only the psychic could see exactly what *would* happen, not a load of fake information which they'd made up on the spot after extracting pieces of information from the client.

"I'd better get some homework done," Daniel muttered, the thoughts having pulled him to a weird place. He wanted to just distract himself, and distracting himself with work seemed like the best option.

After walking into his bedroom, Daniel dropped onto the seat by his desk and pulled the Immunology homework closer, grabbing a pencil and holding it to his mouth almost like a cigarette as he stared at the first, complex equation.

I'm going to come out on the other side as a much better man, he thought, then began to write his answer.

Chapter 6

Daniel leaned back in his chair, pleased with himself. After having handed in his CV to the manager at the restaurant, he was called back for a small interview and told that he'd receive an email if he'd gotten the job. Sure enough, Daniel had just checked his email and there was, right at the top, an email to inform him that he'd been hired.

Daniel let out a light, almost confused breath which teetered within the range of expectance and the range of relief. He'd almost known that he'd get the job. Everything had been exactly the same as when he'd applied before except for the fact that it was a different manager who'd employed him. If he'd done it before, he knew that it would likely for him to have been able to do it again. Still, though, Daniel had felt a small buzz of nerves whenever thinking about the interview and, then, the email which he'd receive to state if he'd been employed or not. He desperately wanted to stick with the job and, at the very least, make it all the way to the end of the school year with the occupation. It just seemed like the right thing to do given that he'd previously been fired.

After standing up and walking into the living area, having woken up and dressed himself in plain, single-coloured clothes only a few minutes before. He wanted to spill the news to his roommates and also to use the bathroom.

The lucky thing was that it was a Saturday, a day off for the majority of the students except for the few who had a single class in the morning. Daniel was one of the students who had an early class, giving him the rest of the day to rest. He'd been informed that he had his first shift in the afternoon the next day, making him quite excited for it. Now that he had the job, Daniel didn't have any nerves regarding anything else to do with it. He'd worked as a waiter in that restaurant before, he technically knew the people whom he'd be working with and he had previous experience, so it wasn't as if there was a reason to be nervous about carrying hot plates around, scared of dropping them. He'd had the practice before.

"I've gotten the job," Daniel stated, walking directly to the bathroom immediately afterwards as he realised that he wouldn't be able to hold it for very long.

"That's great!" The three of them said at the same time or, at least, similar variations of the phrase. Bryan turned to look over the couch.

"You don't sound like you care," he called to Daniel as he closed the bathroom door.

Daniel ignored the statement until he stepped out of the bathroom a few minutes later, having brushed his teeth and washed his face, too.

"Of course I care," he said, his tone making it seem as if Bryan had said that two plus two made five.

"But I've processed it already."

Bryan made a strange clicking noise with his tongue and his teeth, almost like an audio-cue that he was rolling his eyes a little.

"By the way, there's a party going on tonight, apparently," Claire informed, not looking away from the TV which was playing a show which Daniel didn't recognise. "At Henry's place. The three of us are going. Are you?"

Daniel nodded lightly. "Yeah," he stated. Normally, the university wouldn't have liked it very much had someone thrown a party, even a small one, in the provided dormitories. Henry, however, had been saving money since the beginning of his time at high school, never knowing what to spend it on. It just turned out that, on top of the few thousand which his parents lent him for the cause, he had enough to buy a fair-sized apartment in the city. It had been a terrific deal, only so cheap because there were horrible neighbours to the right, left, above and below, but the woman on the left had died and left the apartment empty, the racket-making couple underneath had broken up, leaving the girl to live there on her own, much quieter, and the man to the right had moved out. As a result, the noise-pollution wasn't much of a problem anymore, something which Henry was extremely pleased about as, according to him, it had been like a form of torture to be kept awake until two in the morning when he needed to be up at six to get ready and to the university for an early class.

"Cool, we'll go together at about seven, then."

"Seven?" Daniel questioned, surprised.

"It's going to go until seven in the morning," Bryan elaborated. "Henry decided that he wanted a twelve-hour-long party."

Daniel let out a light breath which could have been interpreted as one of both surprise and full of sneer. "Well, I'll probably be coming back here by three, then. I have a shift in the afternoon."

Derek let out a slightly annoyed sound. "You're not going to turn into one of those people who complain when it's noisy at eight in the evening, are you?"

Daniel gave Derek a look. "Of course not." He paused. "Nine in the evening."

Derek laughed and returned his attention to the TV while Daniel decided that it would be a good idea to catch up on the homework which would be due within a few days while waiting for the time to leave for Immunology, knowing that, on top of going to bed late, he'd have at least a light hangover and then a work shift the next day. He wouldn't be getting anything to do with university done the next day. That much was obvious.

Daniel spent as much time as he could working, getting as much of his homework done as possible until he had to leave for Immunology, getting through the lesson fairly easily. Then, after he'd returned to the dormitory, he'd decided to have a small amount of time off before getting back to working on his homework until he felt burned out. Afterwards, he simply spent time with Derek, Bryan and Claire, passing the time as best as possible while waiting for the clock to strike seven.

As they waited, Daniel, Derek, Bryan and Claire did a myriad of things. They played games, watched TV shows and movies, sometimes just made-up random things to do such as seeing who could do the most press-ups in a row, something which Derek won, Bryan following closely behind, drawing with Claire, then Daniel in last place. They'd all managed to do a similar amount, but that didn't stop jokes about Daniel being weak from being traded every now and then as they waited.

As soon as it turned seven, the four of them grabbed everything which they'd need, then left, leaving the campus and heading in the direction of Henry's apartment alongside a slurry of another hundred people, one of whom, Daniel realised, seeing her in the distance, was Elisha.

The walk was quick. It only ended up taking a few minutes of strolling to reach the apartment building which Henry lived in, something which was to be expected as it wouldn't have been smart for him to get an apartment which was a few miles away from the university.

Everyone piled into the building one after another after Henry had opened the main door to greet them. Henry led them all up the stairs and into his apartment, making sure to tell everyone what the boundaries were: don't trash the place and don't invade his bedroom to have sex. Those were the only two rules, at least the two which weren't obvious and which Henry felt as if he'd needed to voice.

As soon as Daniel walked into the apartment alongside Derek, he almost felt his mood change. It felt as if he'd gone from feeling nonchalant to really... tired. Tired as in drained. Tired as in he really needed to let himself go and have fun, not worry about everything which was going on in his life for once. He'd made sure to prepare so that the next day would be easier. Would there be any harm in drinking more than he usually would?

No, Daniel told himself, knowing that it was a bad idea. He didn't want to slip back into the mindset which he'd used to have. Yes, he was at a party, yes he was going to get drunk and have fun, but he wasn't going to let himself go completely insane.

"I'll get us some drinks," Derek said, patting Daniel on the shoulder to catch his attention in case he couldn't hear the words over the music which, surprisingly, wasn't blaring, more very slightly louder than the limit for it being comfortable.

Looking around himself, Daniel could see a lot of people starting to slip into the atmosphere, almost as if a switch inside of their brains had been flicked and their personalities and moods had immediately shifted. People who, before, may have looked slightly stern, now looked fairly loose and fun. People hadn't begun disbanding and wandering off on their own yet, but Daniel knew that the time would come when people would completely throw caution to the wind and try to mingle with other people, start acting out dangerous stunts for the fun of it, probably fighting someone else because they'd made a move on their partner. For a second, Daniel almost worried that he'd end up like that, but ruled it out. He was calm. He wasn't aggressive. And, anyway, he had a limit. He wasn't going to go crazy, just have some fun.

Derek returned, two cans of beer in his hands. "No cups," he stated, looking pleased. "We get whole cans."

"Thanks, Einstein, I can see that," Daniel joked, sounding almost like Claire, something which Derek noticed and, upon thinking about Claire, started looking around, wondering where she and Bryan had gone. "They've probably gotten closer to the music," Daniel estimated, almost reading Derek's mind. "You know that they like to dance."

"Even though they're terrible at it," Derek mocked, smirking. "I want to see them dance. Come on, let's find them."

Daniel rolled his eyes slightly but, being honest with himself, he didn't want to miss seeing the two of them dancing. They may have thought that they looked cool and admirable but, in all honesty, they both looked as if their bones had been removed and yet they were still trying to move around properly with only muscles.

The two of them began weaving through the still-thickening crowd. The apartment was definitely big enough to fit more than a hundred people inside, so Henry had left the door open for anyone else who

76

wanted to come, something which Daniel was questioning slightly as it was a Saturday and a lot of people would be free. If too many people were going to try to join, there'd probably end up being problems.

It took a minute of searching, but Daniel spotted Bryan and Claire in the corner, the two of them chatting to… Elisha?

"Found them," Daniel mumbled, grabbing Derek's arm and pulling him close enough to be able to point them out. Daniel had no idea that Elisha knew Claire or Bryan, let alone the two of them. It seemed like a weird coincidence.

After heading over, Derek and Daniel were greeted warmly, Elisha giving Daniel a quick hug as she hadn't seen him in person for a while.

"How do you know each other?" Daniel asked Elisha, referring to her relationship with Bryan or Claire.

Elisha took a moment to process the question, but Bryan answered before she had a chance to.

"Didn't she say?" Bryan asked, looking surprised. He elaborated. "I've known Elisha since high school. I know that she's taking the same course as you, so I asked her to keep an eye on you in the lessons and to make sure that you were okay."

Daniel raised his eyebrows slightly, surprised. That made much more sense than Elisha having just decided to give him her number and openly state that she was willing to talk any time. She must have thought that, as Daniel was a friend of Bryan's, he could be a friend of hers, too.

"That makes sense," Daniel said slowly, laughing a little. "It never clicked."

"You two have known each other for... how long?" Claire asked, looking between Elisha and Daniel. "And yet, you never realised *why* you know each other." She snickered slightly. "Can't be a great friendship."

Daniel let out a small breath, knowing that Claire's words weren't meant to be malicious but feeling as if there was *some* type of emotion behind them which wasn't very positive. Either that, or Claire had already managed to get fairly drunk.

"Well," Bryan began, looking almost excited. "I'm going to dance."

"You're not, are you?" Elisha whined.

"Of course I am!"

"Yeah, me too," Claire added, chirping in.

"You know what? I will, too."

Daniel stared at Derek, flabbergasted. "You? Dancing?"

Derek sneered. "I know, I know," he let out. "Might as well try, though. It'll be a laugh."

Daniel considered it for a second. "Fine, I'll join you."

"I'm not missing that," Elisha agreed.

Bryan began walking away. "Let's go centre-stage!"

Daniel and Derek both let out a noise similar to that of a cat being stood on.

"And let everyone see us? Hell no!" Derek

exclaimed, laughing to himself. "I'll watch you up there, but I'm not doing anything."

Bryan looked at Derek, looking almost stern. "I think we should pick him up."

"What?"

"Yeah, let's pick him up and carry him there," Claire added. "Then- Ooo! He can crowd-surf!"

Derek took a step back and shook his head violently. "No, no! I'll dance!"

The five of them ended up simply staying together in their small group, making jokes, dancing to the best of their abilities, though for Daniel and Derek it never progressed to anything more than swerving their bodies around and moving their arms about. Daniel felt incredibly awkward and embarrassed while moving, feeling completely daft. He wasn't built to dance.

Elisha, Claire and Bryan let themselves go probably too much more than necessary. The three of them attracted the attention of others nearby and, after a moment, there must have been ten pairs of eyes watching them dance around, laughing about it but, Daniel could see, the three of them were nervous to be performing.

"We'll get us some more beer!" Derek called to them, then grabbed Daniel's arm and pulled him away, trying to escape from the situation, also trying to hide his laughter as he walked.

"Good thinking," Daniel said while they moved through the crowd and towards the table which had a few boxes of canned beer, a few bottles of wines, vodka, cider, whisky, rum, anything alcoholic, basically. They grabbed five more cans and, as they were about to leave, Henry approached.

"Having fun?" He asked, glancing at the three beers which Derek was holding. "Don't down them all at once. I don't feel like having a chunky carpet."

Derek chuckled. "Getting them for the others."

"Seen their dancing?"

"Of course."

"It's just as horrific as last time."

Oh, yeah, Daniel thought. *Last time.*

A few months before, someone else in the university had held a party in their dorm. It was quite small and it had been kept as secret as possible to keep from the staff finding out. Claire and Bryan had ended up in the spotlight, dancing in front of twenty people who'd been cheering them on. The only catch was that Claire had been so drunk that she'd toppled over and into the crowd and, trying to catch herself with anything, had to resort to stopping the fall by using the girl in front of her, having caught the collar of the girl's shirt, ripping it down the middle and revealing that she hadn't been wearing a bra. It had been a moment which everyone had laughed at, one which had been made even better when the girl had punched Claire so hard in the face that she'd ended up being knocked out. The story ended up being spread throughout the university, even a few of the teachers hearing about it and making a few sarcastic comments to Claire about the situation.

"By the way," Henry continued, pulling the two

of them closer to talk a little more privately. "There's a stripper here."

"What?"

A few whoops came from the other side of the large living room.

"I've gotten us a stripper," Henry repeated, then pulled back, looking smug. "She's going to just set up a pole quickly and start dancing at some random point. Haven't told anyone, so keep it quiet!"

With that, Henry disappeared into the crowd, leaving Derek and Daniel to stand there and look at each other, amused.

"Wonder if she'll do more than stripping," Derek wondered, though Daniel elbowed him in the back as they began walking back to where Claire, Bryan and Elisha were, silently telling him to shut up.

It took a few moments to get back to the others but, once they'd arrived, they saw that the dancing had come to a stop before they handed the drinks out.

"How come you've stopped?" Derek asked, smirking. "Did Claire have another accident?"

"No, we… just got… tired," Bryan spluttered, panting. He took a large swig of beer and took a few deep breaths. "Did you hear the cheering?"

"We did," Daniel confirmed, having wondered slightly what that had been for.

"What's next on the agenda, then?" Derek asked, looking intrigued.

The five of them spent a lot of time together over the following few hours though, by the time it hit eleven, they began to dissipate slightly. Derek disappeared to see the stripper after hearing that she was putting on a show, leaving the others alone. Daniel would have gone normally but wasn't in the mood, and the others weren't interested in seeing a woman taking her clothes off and swinging around a pole.

The next to leave had been Claire as she'd ended up being approached by an extraordinarily tall and handsome boy who'd ended up flirting with her and subsequently dragging her away to somewhere. Bryan then ended up disappearing at midnight, having stumbled across Jacob, wanting to spend some time with his boyfriend, leaving Daniel and Elisha alone.

The two of them sat on the ground on one, far side of the living room, their backs pressed against a wall, drinks still in their hands. Daniel had lost count as to how many drink's he'd had at that point, but knew that he was drunk. He was drunk enough to feel woozy and notice a significant decrease in how much he was taking in when looking at something, but he wasn't drunk enough to start acting out of the ordinary or not to acknowledge that he was drunk. Elisha, too, was experiencing a few effects, something which she'd voiced to him, stating that she'd noticed that her head kept tilting to the left if she tried to keep it still and pointed straight up.

Having spent a few hours at the party already, Daniel had experienced two things which stood out to him. One of the things which he'd remembered he'd experienced at a party before as the moment occurred

82

was that he was offered some marijuana and, then, once Daniel had declined, thinking bitterly about the fact that he'd lost his job in the real world because someone had framed him as the owner of the same drug, was offered cigarettes, reminding Daniel that, before the lucid dream had began, he'd been addicted to smoking, at least to the extent that he'd have at least six or seven cigarettes a day. He had a decent amount of willpower, meaning that he never truly ended up as addicted as people can get with certain, nicotine-filled things, but he couldn't quit. After getting into the lucid dream however, Daniel could only guess that he'd been so distracted that he simply didn't feel the craving for a while and then, mystically, it was gone. It had probably happened as he'd been distracted and as he was asleep, his brain probably able to control if he'd feel certain cravings or not a lot better than in the real world.

After having been offered drugs and tobacco, Daniel ended up stumbling across the sight of a girl trying to, or, at least, it appeared as if she were trying to, pressure another girl into doing something, something which Daniel didn't know the extent of, but something which he could tell was making the other girl very uncomfortable. Daniel ended up discreetly watching for a minute before intervening, stepping in when the pushy girl started to also become the grabby girl. He ended up getting punched by that girl, then hugged by the other girl, then left alone to debate with himself whether or not his jaw had loosened slightly. The event had made him feel slightly proud of himself as he'd realised that, before, he may have just ignored the situation. He'd been a push-over with his friends and family and, on top of that, he'd hated all types of conflict. He could hear someone say something racist and crave to be able to get himself to explain why it wasn't right, yet he couldn't muster the courage to do so, usually ending up listening to someone else doing the explaining while he'd silently beat himself up over the fact that he didn't have any guts.

Elisha began to lean her head on the wall behind her. "This is sort of boring now, isn't it?" She asked. Daniel glanced at her and she quickly edited the statement. "Not because we're alone! I mean, it's kind of dragged out, you know?"

Daniel chuckled. "I know what you mean," he replied, then looked at her properly. "Want to get out of here?"

Elisha gave him a funny look. "Where will we go?" She questioned. "It's eleven in the evening." She slurred the word "the" and tried to stop herself from giggling at that.

"We can go back to my dorm," Daniel said, testing the waters.

Elisha considered it, then nodded. "Okay," she said before standing up, spilling a little of her beer onto the carpet as she did so. "Whoops."

"All the more reason to get out fast," Daniel muttered, Elisha barely able to hear him over the still slightly loud music, but she laughed at the statement.

The two of them finished their drinks quickly

and dropped the cans into a bin on their way out of the door, heading down the stairs and onto the street outside.

The cold air smacked Daniel in the face and made him realise that spending a lot of time in a room with a lot of people was going to make the air very humid. He hadn't even realised that he'd been lightly sweating from the warmth of the air in the room. Had a window been open at all throughout that party?

They walked back in the direction of the university, both of them still sober enough to be able to more or less walk in straight lines, though, occasionally, they'd sway a little and lose their balance. At one point, Elisha swayed at the perfect time to walk into a lamppost, then Daniel did the same, walking into a bin and almost falling over it.

The two of them made it back to the campus alive and entered the building, heading up the stairs and to the seventh floor. Daniel had to remind Elisha that she wasn't going to her room as she'd almost walked onto the fourth floor, to which she'd stated that it was simply habit.

As soon as the two of them had made it into Daniel's dormitory, they stood in the living area. Everything around them was quiet. It felt strange to be inside *and* in silence.

"Okay, so what do we do?" Daniel questioned, looking at Elisha. She shrugged lazily, then headed to where she guessed was the bathroom, saying that she'd be out in a moment.

Daniel leaned against the back of the couch, slightly surprised with himself. If someone had told him that he'd end up very easily asking Elisha back to his dormitory, he wouldn't have believed it. It almost seemed as if he'd asked her there to spend some alone time with her and, to Daniel, alone time mixed with being drunk seemed like a slightly dangerous combination.

It took two minutes for Elisha to walk out of the bathroom. She almost tripped while heading over to Daniel, the two of them laughing about it.

"There are a few beers in the fridge," Daniel stated, remembering as he said the words. "Want one?"

"Sure," Elisha replied. She flopped onto the couch while Daniel walked over to the fridge and pulled out two canned beers. He popped the tops of both, headed back to Elisha and gave her one. She took a sip. "I definitely prefer this brand."

Daniel laughed a little, dropping onto the couch without spilling the beer, something which surprised him slightly. He took a sip. "The stuff which Henry had is the cheap stuff," he explained. "Probably didn't want to spend a fortune on stuff for other people."

They went quiet for a moment. The two of them put their cans on the coffee table. Daniel let out a small sigh, content.

"Hey," Elisha started, looking at him. "Is it weird that we're here alone?"

Daniel raised his eyebrows slightly, not looking at her. He grabbed his beer again and took another swig.

86

"I don't think so," he stated, placing the drink back onto the table. "Why?"

"Well, *anything* could happen," she continued. "We're here, drinking, already sort of drunk." As if to prove her point, she slurred slightly and laughed. "You could probably kiss me, and I wouldn't push you away even if I don't like you like that."

"Do you like me like that?"

Elisha considered it for a moment. "Never thought about it," she said, then took a long swig of her drink. Once she'd put it down, she turned back to him. "So, are you going to kiss me?"

Daniel let out a nervous breath, then bit his tongue lightly. "I don't know," he admitted. "Maybe, maybe not."

"You don't know?"

"No, I don't know."

Elisha positioned her lips slightly, almost making it look as if she were pouting as she thought.

"Are you going to kiss me?" Daniel asked, turning the question on her.

"I don't know," Elisha stated. "Maybe, maybe not."

The two of them stared at each other for a few moments, then burst out laughing. It was almost as if they couldn't take each other seriously. Why were they talking about kissing each other? If they were going to do it, they'd just do it, not talk about it.

Elisha leaned in and gave Daniel a quick kiss on the cheek. "That's the most you're getting," she stated, sounding proud. "Happy with that?"

Daniel stared at her for a moment, dumbfounded as he hadn't expected anything like that. "Yeah," he said. "Happy with that."

The two of them drank more until they finished their cans. Daniel stood up and got two more from the fridge.

Chapter 7

Daniel woke up without opening his eyes and could immediately feel the headache. He let out a groan, rolling over in the bed, moving a hand to clutch his right temple. He'd known that he'd end up feeling so disgusting, yet he'd continued drinking anyway. At that moment, Daniel didn't hate anything more than himself.

For a few moments, Daniel braced himself for the moment when he'd open his eyes. He knew from experience that he'd open his eyes and any light would penetrate his retinas with the intent to torture him. He took a moment to take a deep breath, then slowly opened his right eye before biting the bullet and popping them both open.

Daniel let out another groan, but he continued to look around at his room. At least he'd found his way to bed alright. He wouldn't have been surprised had he ended up sleeping on the floor.

Why was there a hand on his chest?

Daniel looked over and realised that Elisha was sound asleep next to him, looking so peaceful that he could have believed her to have been in some sort of coma.

"Oh, God," Daniel muttered, pulling away from her, scooting closer to his bedside table. He realised that his alarm hadn't gone off and, after checking why, saw that he'd disabled it the night before. How had he thought to disable the alarm clock? It was almost eleven in the morning, giving him four hours before his shift. He'd be able to treat the hangover within that time. Well, hopefully after dealing with Elisha.

Daniel looked back at her. Her wavy, black hair was sticking up in places, less wavy, frizzier and a lot messier. It was plastered to parts of her face and neck and shoulders and, oh, God, she was naked.

After checking, Daniel realised that he was, too.

Brilliant, Daniel thought, sarcastic even in his own head. He leaned back into the pillow, closing his eyes for a moment.

What could he do? Would it be wise to wake her? Wouldn't it be a bit too much for her to take in all at once? First waking up and feeling the pain of the hangover, then realising that she was with Daniel, then having to theorise about why they were both naked and in bed together, something which wouldn't take much figuring out but would supply a healthy dose of embarrassment.

Daniel glanced at her face, taking care as to only look at her face, trying to figure out if it would be okay to wake her. Wait! What if he could set the alarm clock and have *that* wake her up? Then, after setting the alarm, he could go to the bathroom, allow her to adjust to everything properly and, then, once he'd get back, he'd be up and dressed. That would quench some of the embarrassment, right? Surely it would.

After considering his options, Daniel decided that he didn't have a better plan. He reached over to the alarm clock and set the alarm for eleven, then immediately forced himself out of the bed, nearly collapsing to the ground when the pain which his headache was causing him spiked drastically, though he managed to stabilise himself and sweep some clothes from the floor, not recognising them as the clothes which he'd worn the day before, having to make sure that he wasn't putting any of Elisha's clothes on by mistake.

Daniel ended up taking three minutes just trying to pull his clothes on. He didn't want to leave even a part of his body unclothed, making sure to pull socks on, even his trainers after a moment of consideration. With his shoes, he wouldn't have as much of an urge to get back into the bed as he'd have to wrestle to get them back on afterwards, and there was no chance of wearing shoes on his bed. That would keep him up later on, saving him from possibly jolting awake with five minutes before his shift and a need to rush around to prepare.

Daniel glanced at the alarm clock. He had a minute to get out of the room before the alarm would go off. After that, Elisha would be awake, and Daniel definitely didn't want to be there to see her moment of realisation when she'd process that she wasn't in *her* room.

After stumbling to the door, Daniel managed to get into the main living area and close the door behind him. Then, straight away, his mind switched to focus on one thing: water.

Daniel rushed to the sink, grabbed a drinking glass and filled it with ice-cold water from the tap, proceeding to down the contents of the glass within seconds, refill the glass, then drink all of the water. Next thing: coffee.

After filling the kettle and turning it on, Daniel grabbed a mug from the cupboard and dropped two tablespoons of grounded coffee into the bottom of the mug. No sugar. No milk. He wanted it to be so strong that it would jar the headache out of him.

Right, Daniel thought. *Bathroom, then Elisha.*

Daniel headed to the bathroom and, as he closed the door, heard his alarm clock beginning to beep. It was muffled, something which was fortunate as Daniel didn't want to wake anyone else up. Well, if they were even there. There was always the possibility that they'd gone off and ended up staying with someone else, maybe ended up falling asleep somewhere in Henry's apartment. Daniel hoped so. He didn't want to have to see the looks on their faces when they'd see that Elisha had been sleeping with him.

After using the toilet quickly, Daniel made sure to wash his face with the coldest water which the tap would let out, rubbing it in as much as possible, hoping that it would help to wake him up enough. He felt slightly tired but, at the very least, he wouldn't for long. Not with that coffee which was waiting for him.

Daniel brushed his teeth and walked out of the

bathroom. The alarm had turned off. That was one thing.

The kettle had finished boiling and, after a moment of consideration, Daniel wondered if Elisha would like a coffee or not. He didn't know if she drank the stuff but, then again, would she care if it would help with the hangover?

Daniel made his own coffee, then made a much lighter one. He didn't know how she'd take it, so he played it safe with a single teaspoon of sugar and a splash of milk, hoping that it would be okay. Then, bracing himself for the conversation which would greet him within a few moments, took the drinks to his room, pushing the door open.

Elisha darted back into the bed, having managed to grab her underwear and her t-shirt from the floor, fiddling to pull them on, looking extremely uncomfortable.

"Hey," Daniel let out, hearing in his own voice that he was nervous. "I've brought you a coffee."

"Oh, right. Thanks," Elisha let out, trying to avoid eye-contact. She stared at the duvet as Daniel walked around the bed and placed it on her bedside table.

Daniel took a long gulp of his drink, not caring that it scolded his tongue, just wanting the caffeine. "So, I don't think we need to question what happened."

Elisha glanced up at him as he sat down on the edge of the bed, turned to look at her. At least the portion of her body which wasn't hidden by the duvet was covered decently.

"No, we don't," she agreed, sounding embarrassed. She took a long sip of her coffee. "We had sex, right?"

Daniel winced slightly. It was one thing to acknowledge it, but it was another thing to just say it out loud.

"Yeah, probably," he replied, shrugging as if they didn't have all of the clues which pointed towards that being the only logical scenario. "So-"

"We don't need to be awkward with each other," Elisha cut across, sounding slightly unsure but trying to sound confident with her words. "We had sex. So what? Friends do that all the time."

"Really?" Daniel questioned, close to looking at her but forcing himself to look away. He was too embarrassed to look at her. "Derek hasn't made any moves," he joked, then took a long sip of his coffee, feeling the liquid burn his mouth slightly.

The two of them quieted for a moment. "You know what I mean," Elisha concluded meekly. "We got drunk and curious, I guess. It happens all the time to loads of people."

"Yeah, I guess."

They quieted again, though, after a moment, Elisha let out a small sigh, almost sounding disappointed. "This isn't going to affect our friendship," she stated, sounding sure of herself. She didn't even sound questioning, not as if she were asking a question, seeing if Daniel felt the same, simply saying it, knowing it to be the truth.

"No, it isn't," Daniel agreed, feeling as if he was lying slightly but trying not to focus on that thought. "It'll only affect the friendship if we *let* it affect the friendship."

Elisha winced slightly and grabbed her head, then took a long gulp of the drink in her hands.

"Well, I'll leave you to get dressed," Daniel said before standing up, quickly walking towards the door.

"Daniel," Elisha called, making him stop in his tracks.

Daniel turned and looked at her, questioning what she wanted to add.

"I'll be out in a minute."

Daniel left the room and closed the door, letting out a long sigh.

Once Elisha had finished getting dressed and had walked out of Daniel's bedroom, the two of them spent a few minutes trying to figure out what had happened between them and how they'd arrived at the situation which they were in. Daniel could remember taking her back to the dorm but couldn't remember much after that. There were a few vague memories of the two of them sitting down and trying to play a game, then an extremely hazy memory of Elisha making the first move, having moved in to kiss him, but he couldn't remember anything else afterwards. Elisha could vaguely remember that, at one point, she'd rushed to the bathroom to throw up, but that was it. She couldn't even pinpoint when that would have happened! The two of them were in the dark, essentially, only knowing where they'd ended up but clueless as to the journey which led them there.

After having tried to figure everything out, the two of them worked together, trying to get over their hangovers as much as possible. The two of them ended up drinking another mug of extremely strong coffee each alongside three, tall glasses of ice-cold water, hoping that there would be an effect. There was, in the end, as Daniel's headache ended up numbing slightly, the pain reducing to a much more manageable point, though it still wasn't pleasant. Elisha suggested that it would be a good idea for them to shower, stating how the steam would probably help them, but she ended up wording the sentence wrong and causing a slight amount of awkward tension to fill the atmosphere until she corrected herself.

Elisha ended up leaving at half-eleven, wanting to get back to her dorm in case her roommates were worrying, though, in reality, Daniel knew that she just wanted to get away from him, the feeling mutual. He almost felt stupid, almost felt as if he'd managed to fall down the stairs in front of dozens of people. He felt as if he could have avoided the situation had he been more careful, felt embarrassed, awkward and, most of all, weakened.

Daniel had a shower as Elisha had suggested, then walked out of the bathroom to find that Bryan was up, making himself a coffee.

"Morning," he croaked, seeing Daniel's reflection in the black, glossy coating of the kettle.

"Morning," Daniel replied, his voice much better than Bryan's, making him wonder just what had happened at the party after he'd left.

"What happened last night?" Bryan questioned, turning around to face Daniel while waiting for the kettle to boil. He began leaning on the countertop, looking at Daniel, intrigued. "You and Elisha just disappeared last night."

Daniel paused for a moment, debating inwardly whether or not it would be wise to tell Bryan about what had happened. Though, in all fairness, Bryan and Elisha *did* know each other very well, anyway, so he was bound to find out at some point, either from him or from Elisha.

"We came back here," Daniel explained, wanting to keep his answer vague, though Bryan raised an eyebrow, his eyes widening slightly.

"Tell me more," he urged, hearing the click of the kettle which signified that the water had finished boiling.

Daniel let out a little sigh, trying to think of how to word his explanation without making it blatantly obvious. "Well, we started to find the party boring, so we came back here to hang out."

"And?" Bryan pushed as he poured the water into a mug. "Did anything happen?"

"We may have slept together," Daniel said, quietly and quickly, hoping that Bryan wouldn't understand what he'd said, though Bryan span around and stared at Daniel, his mouth agape.

"What?" He let out, shocked. "You slept together?" He repeated. He looked at the ground as he pieced everything together in his mind. "As in literally, or as in you had sex?"

"Maybe both," Daniel admitted, still unsure but knowing the answer deep down.

Bryan laughed lightly, under his breath but loud enough for Daniel to be able to hear the sound of bewilderment in his tone. "Wow," he simply stated, turning around to finish making his coffee. "Did you decide to?"

"We were both drunk," Daniel stated.

"How drunk?"

"Pissed," Daniel admitted, chuckling slightly. "So drunk that I can barely remember anything."

Bryan whistled slightly. "How is she?"

"What are you, a doctor?" Daniel asked rhetorically, amused. "As in, how's she feeling about it?"

Bryan nodded.

"Well, she finds it sort of funny, I suppose," Daniel recalled. "She said that a lot of friends end up doing it when they get drunk, so she wasn't very bothered."

"I suppose she's just glad that she can't remember it."

"Hey! I'm not that bad!"

Bryan laughed, placed the kettle back onto the stand, tossed the teaspoon into the sink, picked the mug up and turned around, taking a sip. "I'll just have to take your word for it, I suppose."

Daniel rolled his eyes slightly. "So, what happened with you and Jacob?"

"Take a guess."

Daniel knew immediately, so he didn't bother pushing for more information.

"Well, I'm going back to bed," Bryan stated, beginning to walk back to his room.

"With a coffee?" Daniel questioned, confused. "Is it decaf, or something?"

"No, I'm just going back to bed," Bryan said. "I'm going to have a lazy day. This is just for the headache," he explained, holding the mug up slightly while talking about it. "Bye." And, with that, he walked into his room and closed the door, leaving Daniel on his own.

Daniel spent three and a half hours relaxing, sitting in his room on his computer, passing the time until there were only five minutes before his shift was due to start. Initially, he'd considered getting a small amount of work done, relaxing and then getting to work early, thinking that it would be beneficial to both use some of time productively and to get to the restaurant early to show initiative, but he'd ended up giving up, not wanting to push himself too hard with work out of fear of making his headache worse due to stress. It wasn't nearly as bad as it had been upon waking up, but it definitely wasn't gone. Daniel could barely distract himself from the constant, sharp ache in his skull.

As soon as he saw the time, he left the dormitory,

heading down the stairs, out of the building and then off the campus and into the city, heading towards the restaurant.

The walk was brisk, Daniel making sure not to be late, arriving at the restaurant a minute before his shift would officially start.

After walking in, Daniel was greeted by the manager and, he realised, Dale, the manager whom he'd been working under, was still only a trainee.

"So, this is how it's going to work," the other manager said, beginning to lead Daniel and Dale to the back room of the restaurant, her office, presumably. They walked into the room which Daniel had forgotten a lot about. There was a small, cramped desk with an old computer and monitor barely able to fit on one side of it with a miniscule amount of space left over for the keyboard. There were a few, rickety yet comfortable chairs in the corner, one of them with a folded pile of clothes which Daniel knew he'd be donning within minutes. "You're going to change into those in the bathroom, then we're going to give you a notepad and a pen and we're going to observe you waiting on a table, got it?"

Daniel nodded, slightly enthusiastic. He already knew the gist of what would be happening as he'd done it all before, but he was curious to see how his skills were. It had been at least two and a half years since he'd last waited on a table. Had his blade been rusted?

The manager scooped the uniform off of the chair and into her arms, proceeding to hand it to Daniel.

"The bathrooms are close-by," she said. "Just bring the clothes which you're wearing back here. Oh, and, by the way, you'll be coming to work in that from now on."

Daniel nodded, then left the room, heading to the bathrooms. He stood in a stall for two minutes, awkwardly changing into the uniform with confined space, eventually managing it. He stepped out of the stall and gazed at himself in the mirror, feeling nostalgic to be dressed that way again. It felt amazing. It almost felt as if he was getting a grip on his life. It felt as if he'd gotten a new job in the real world.

Daniel left the bathroom and returned to the office, dumping the clothes which he'd previously been wearing onto the chair, giving them a look afterwards which could have suggested that he thought of them as dirty and disgusting.

The manager looked at him, then walked around him, checking for anything which was out of place. After returning to the spot in front of him, she gave him a simple, impressed nod.

"Good," she said, then grabbed a notepad and a pen from her desk, thrusting them into Daniel's hands. "Walk around, get a good idea of the layout and wait on the first table which you find."

"Aren't I supposed to be given a section?" Daniel questioned, smiling inwardly at the shocked and impressed look on the two manager's faces.

"Usually, yes," she admitted, moving her head to the side quite harshly as if trying to nod while breaking her neck. "But, just for now and so that we can see how you handle the customers, you're free to go anywhere in the restaurant. It's not very big, anyway. It's not as if you'll get lost."

Daniel smirked slightly at the thought of somehow getting lost while looking for a table to wait on, like he'd be on a dangerous quest, hunting for long-lost treasure, having gotten lost in a deep ravine with no way out.

After a moment of looking at the notepad and the pen, Daniel turned and walked out of the door, heading to the dining area, the two managers following him. Dale had been told to supervise Daniel, no doubt, in order to train Dale for future training tasks.

It took a minute for a table to call Daniel over and, when he approached the tall, friendly-looking bald man and who must have been his elderly mother, Daniel felt a wave of almost excitement and nervousness. "Hi, what can I get you?" Daniel asked with a smile, noticing that the tone of his voice was exactly the same as it had been when he'd worked there previously. He flicked the notepad open with the thumb of his left hand and clicked the pen, holding it close to the paper, ready to write.

"I'll have the spaghetti," the bald man said.

"And I'll have the lasagne," the lady added.

"Even the dishes are related," Daniel joked, making the bald man chuckle under his breath and making the woman almost grin, amused. Daniel quickly finished writing the orders on the notepad. "Any drinks?"

"No, thank you," the bald man concluded,

giving Daniel a quick smile.

Daniel returned the smile, turning and walking right past the managers, tearing the page out of the notepad, hanging it just on the top lip of the split wall which allowed some visual into the kitchen.

"That was great!" The manager stated, catching Daniel's attention. He turned and looked at her, then managed a light smile.

"Thanks," he said.

The manager clapped her hands together once, quite lightly, then held her combined hands to her chin, poking the end of her nose with the tips of her pressed-together middle fingers. "We'll assign you a section and we'll keep an eye on you for the rest of the day," she said, flicking her wrists forward. "By the looks of things, you don't need any training, but we'll evaluate you properly for the rest of the day to see if there's anything to refine."

She turned and looked at the room. "You take that quarter," she said after a moment, gesturing towards the far, right corner of the room. There must had been at least five or six tables there, a decent number of chairs connected to them. "I'll find the others and let them know that you're dealing with that section," she added, looking back to Daniel as if waiting for his approval or acknowledgment.

As Daniel looked at his new section, he felt a mixture of a sudden pang of excitement and determination, hoping that he'd be able to do a sufficient-enough job to impress the manager.

"You should take some time between the next few shifts to learn the menu, by the way, but you should be able to get through today without knowing it off-by-heart," she added, the speed and tone of her voice making it sound as if she'd only just remembered to mention it.

Daniel nodded lightly, respectfully. The manager clapped him on the shoulder lightly.

"Get back to work, then," she said, then turned and stood by the wall, watching Daniel as he wandered off to search his section for people needing a waiter.

Chapter 8

A handful of days passed quickly. Daniel managed to settle into his job properly after his first shift, and he'd had two more and had begun to get to know his co-workers again. The manager had left, leaving Dale in charge, making Daniel feel as if he was starting to fit in even more as it was becoming closer to what he was used to.

Bryan had ended up telling Derek and Claire that Daniel and Elisha had spent the night together, and they both used it as an opportunity to tease him as much as humanly possible. Derek would constantly make remarks, always something on the lines of "the two training scientists exploring biology." Daniel didn't mind the teasing very much, finding it funnier than he found it annoying, but it reminded him that he and Elisha hadn't seen each other properly, or, at least, they hadn't spent any time together outside of seeing each other in lessons since the incident. Daniel and Elisha had also only talked a little since their incident, but Elisha had suddenly decided that she wanted to see him, having sent a quick text to tell him to be awake and out of bed at a decent time before classes that day.

Daniel was up, pulling the same clothes on from the day before, when Elisha sent him another text, telling him that she'd be there within a few minutes.

Daniel didn't have to get out of bed any earlier than usual, but he didn't like the fact that he didn't have the option to stay in bed and relax for a little longer. He was exhausted as, the previous day, it seemed as if all of his teachers had flung extensive homework at their students and had demanded the papers to be turned in by the next lesson. Daniel had two, long lessons that day, and the day before, he'd spent at least three hours on each piece of homework, trying to perfect it for the next day. He didn't feel so tired that he couldn't think straight or even that he couldn't move very much without passing out, but he was definitely a bit grouchy.

After getting dressed, then quickly going to the bathroom to brush his teeth, Daniel sat in the living area, waiting for Elisha to show up. Bryan had been there before but, once Daniel had explained what was happening, he'd decided to retreat, telling Daniel that he wanted to give the two of them space as the conversation was no doubt going to be extremely awkward.

Daniel sat in the living area, waiting, pondering just what Elisha wanted to talk about. Part of his mind wondered whether or not she was going to want to discuss what had happened, whether or not they'd had sex or not despite the fact that, as Daniel saw it, they'd already concluded that they had. Then, with a sudden stroke of fear, Daniel wondered if she'd ended up getting pregnant. Surely that hadn't happened, right? She hadn't gotten pregnant. They *were* drunk, but both of them wouldn't have neglected protection, right?

Right?

Daniel began to sweat slightly, feeling the back of his t-shirt start to become slightly damp. He seriously hoped that he hadn't just jeopardized his chances of fixing his university year. All he wanted was the satisfaction of completing the year without ending it while feeling traumatised by events. He didn't want to end it having been fired from a job, so he was going to get to the end without being fired. He didn't want to end the year having failed to get his PhD again, so he wasn't going to fail. But was he going to be able to fix everything properly with a baby on the way? He didn't want to have to technically cheat reality by undoing anything which had gone wrong. Even though he had the power to, Daniel didn't want to just skip to the end of the year and have his PhD and be happy. He wanted the full experience. But how hellish would the experience be with a baby?

A knock came from the door. Daniel jumped off of the couch and bolted to it, pulling the door open to see Elisha. She looked fine. She didn't look very shocked, not even embarrassed, so Daniel guessed that she wasn't going to dump a heavy confession on him. She couldn't have been pregnant, surely. His mind had simply taken the idea and had ran into the distance with it, frolicking through grass, knocking worry-laced pollen back to him with enough of it to make him violently sneeze a new fear into his mind.

"So…" Daniel began, letting the word drag on. "Come in!" He gestured behind himself and laughed nervously.

"You don't need to be so awkward," Elisha assured him, looking slightly amused. "There's nothing big to tell you, I'm not pregnant or dying, or anything. I just want to discuss."

Daniel let out a small, relieved breath.

The two of them moved to the couch and sat next to each other. Daniel noticed that Elisha seemed unusually comfortable with sitting right next to him, her left thigh pushing into his right, their shoulders brushing against each other.

"So, about us," Elisha began, gazing at him, a light smile on her face. "I've been thinking and, honestly, I think I know why what happened ended up happening."

"Go on," Daniel urged, intrigued. The conversation had taken a direction which he hadn't expected at all. As soon as Elisha had said that there wasn't anything major to load off and onto him, Daniel felt relaxed but questioned what the conversation was *actually* going to be about. Why request to see him if it wasn't such a big deal, especially after the two of them had been much more distant than usual over the previous few days? It sparked a wonder in Daniel's mind which made him almost itch for information.

"Well, when we met," Elisha began explaining, pausing slightly, maybe thinking about how to word the sentence. "I thought that you were quite… cute?"

Daniel let out a small, nervous chuckle and leaned back. "You don't need to question it. Of course I
108

am."

Elisha rolled her eyes slightly. "Well, yeah. We started talking and I started thinking that you're quite sweet and funny and kind and-"

Daniel held his hand up slightly, Elisha noticing and stopping her sentence. "What you're saying is that you were attracted to me, at least slightly, and that's what influenced the events, right?"

Elisha stared at him, looking slightly stunned, but she gave a light nod after a moment, the waves in her hair rippling slightly with the movement. "Yeah," she confirmed, her voice slightly quiet.

Daniel gave a weak sort of smile, not sure what to say. He'd just gotten out of a relationship with Laura which, when thinking about it, he was probably over almost entirely. But the big problem which had caused him to end up getting fired and caused him to fail his PhD was the fact that he'd been smothered, essentially. Laura had almost hoarded him as much as possible, had sometimes guided and had sometimes pressured him into making a decision which would result in the two of them spending much more time together. If Daniel was going to fix the problems which had arisen in the year, getting into another relationship would probably just hinder his attempts.

"I had a small crush on you, essentially," Elisha admitted, spelling it out as if Daniel hadn't caught on to what she was trying to say.

"Had?" Daniel questioned, surprised by the use of the past tense. Why admit to a crush which had faded, especially given that they'd just been through an awkward event? Wouldn't admitting that, during that night, she'd liked him just make it even more embarrassing for both of them?

Elisha moved her head to the right side, tilting it slightly, looking as if she was trying to figure out a complicated equation. "Well, yes and no."

Daniel raised his eyebrows slightly, trying to figure out what she was trying to get at.

"Well, I had a tiny crush on you, I suppose, but I don't know how I feel now," she explained, trying her best to wrap everything up, to come to some form of conclusion which would aid the two of them in figuring out just where their relationship stood.

"Okay," Daniel let out, pausing for a moment, taking a deep breath. "Do you still think that I'm cute?"

"Yes," Elisha replied with only a very slight amount of hesitation.

"Do you think that I'm kind?"

"One of the kindest people I know," Elisha replied, pausing slightly after saying it, looking a little shocked with herself.

"Do you think that I'm funny?"

Elisha considered it for a moment. "Sometimes," she stated, ignoring the slight look of hurt which appeared on Daniel's face as she continued. "But I don't know if that's going to tell us anything. I might think those things about you, but that doesn't mean that I have a crush on you," she explained, sounding as if she was making things up as she was going along, trying to get *some* sort of conclusion which wouldn't be embarrassing.

Daniel let out a slight sigh, having hoped that they'd be able to put a stop to the conversation. It hadn't started off very bad, but it had definitely escalated to the point where he was slightly uncomfortable and embarrassed.

"Look," Elisha began, looking at Daniel with a face which almost made her seem pitying. "I think you're a great guy, but I don't know if I like you as anything more than a friend."

"Hold on," Daniel began, confused. "I never-"

Elisha held her hand up in front of her as she continued, completely neglecting what Daniel was saying. "I'll have a think about it, I suppose, and I'll tell you what I can figure out."

Daniel stared at her, waiting for her to finish talking. "Why are you making it sound as if I've asked you out?" He questioned, extremely bewildered.

Elisha tilted her head again, looking like a confused puppy. "I'm not trying to," she admitted, giggling slightly. "I just... I don't know if we can go on as friends if I end up making things awkward."

"What are you talking about?" Daniel questioned, feeling slightly scared that he was going to lose their friendship just because of a drunken night. "We can go on! We can definitely go on!"

Elisha gave him an embarrassed and sorry look. "I'm sorry, Daniel, but I don't think *I* can."

Daniel stared at her, his mouth agape. He wanted

to try to convince her but knew not to. If she wanted to make that decision, she could.

Elisha stood up and began walking to the door.

"Wait!" Daniel called, making her stop in her tracks and turn around. "Don't-"

Elisha laughed a little and sighed, seeming relieved. "Thanks for not letting me go," she said, confusing Daniel more.

"Huh?" Daniel asked, his face looking as if he'd just seen someone defying gravity. "What…"

Elisha returned to him, sitting on the arm of the couch just a few inches away.

"You didn't let me go," she stated. "You value our friendship."

"Well, yeah-"

"How much do you value it?"

Daniel stared at her, extremely taken aback. "Um," he said, trying to calculate exactly how he felt about their friendship. "A lot, I suppose."

Elisha looked satisfied with that answer. "So, you're comfortable with me?"

"Yes?" Daniel replied, trying to urge her to explain what was going on, what the point of bluffing walking away was, why she was asking these questions.

Elisha smiled lightly, then put an arm around Daniel's shoulders and pulled him closer, his head just at the top of her ribs underneath her arm. "I wasn't going to leave," she admitted. "I wanted to see if you were going to stop me."

"Why?" Daniel asked, not objecting to the

sideways hug in the slightest.

"Well, not stopping me means that you value our friendship, and you've just admitted that you value it a lot," Elisha recapped, only making Daniel question the point even more. "You're comfortable with me, so I don't see why there's any reason for us to be awkward if we go on a date."

"A date?" Daniel let out, pulling away to look at her in the eyes. "Since when are we-"

"The Saturday after this one?" She asked, analysing the look on Daniel's face. "Do you want to go on a date with me next Saturday?"

Daniel looked at her for a moment. "Okay," he replied after a second. What would the harm be? Maybe he'd been thinking that a relationship would end up suffocating him even more, but Elisha seemed like a smart and considerate girl. Not to mention that they were taking the same course, studying for the same PhD. They'd be able to help each other, so spending a little extra time together wouldn't be the worst, would it? Daniel didn't think that it would. And, anyway, wouldn't it be beneficial to have someone helping to guide him through the rest of the year? They were getting on well, they'd be able to help each other. What was the harm?

Elisha smiled, then pulled Daniel back in for a quick hug before she scooted off of the arm of the couch. "Our first lesson's in an hour," she explained. "I'd better go and get ready for it."

Daniel nodded lightly before standing up too,

walking Elisha to the door as if he were returning her to her home after a date. "See you in an hour, then," he said.

Elisha gave a quick nod and a smile before she walked out of the dormitory and Daniel closed the door after her.

Fifty-five minutes passed until Daniel had decided that it was time to leave for Virology. He grabbed his bag and left his dorm, heading to the class. He'd been occasionally thinking about what was going on with Elisha and, the more that he thought about the situation, the more that he realised that he really didn't mind the idea of a date. It would be the first date with a new girl for him in three years, more or less, and given what had happened with Laura both in his head and in reality, Daniel guessed that dating another girl would really help with his mental state. It would provide a distraction from the catastrophe which had been his and Laura's relationship.

Daniel walked into the Virology class and found his way to his seat, passing in front of Elisha as he did so.

As Daniel passed in front of her, she tapped him in the back of his left calf with her foot, making him look at her, slightly scared as he hadn't expected the touch. Elisha only giggled under her breath, a hand covering her mouth, before she pulled her hand away, smiled at him, then nodded in the direction of Daniel's seat, telling him to go and sit down.

Daniel complied, taking his seat, amused. It

wouldn't be a bad thing to have someone like her more prominent in his life. He knew that for a fact.

The day breezed by, Daniel trying his best to focus on the work presented to him, but he would occasionally lose a bit of focus, wondering what he and Elisha would do for their date. At one point, it hit him that he was thinking along the lines of a lovestruck romantic when, in fact, the occasion would only be slightly more than two friends spending some time together while doing... something which he hadn't figured out yet. He made a mental note of the fact that it would be best to organise what they'd be doing as soon as possible lest they would, or at least, *he* would, just end up stressing himself out over the ordeal.

The rest of the day passed without much going on, Daniel only pummelling through each lesson and duelling any distracting thoughts which would suddenly appear, until Daniel returned to his dormitory, checked his phone just after having entered the living area, and noticed that he'd received a text from a childhood friend whom he hadn't spoken to in a long, long time.

Hey, Dan. I'm free this Saturday. Want to hang out?

Daniel looked at the message and felt a smirk growing on his face. Then he remembered that the same childhood friend was due to die on the Sunday, the day right after they'd be seeing each other if Daniel would decide to visit.

Daniel knew that he couldn't pass up the opportunity. He'd previously decided to blow off the chance to see his friend of many years, spending the day with Laura instead, only to find out the next day that Austin had died.

Yeah, of course! I'll meet with you on Saturday in the afternoon. I have a few lessons in the morning, so I should be there at about 3?

Daniel read the message again before sending it, feeling a strange feeling in his chest. Was it sadness mixed with something else, or was it something completely different? Daniel couldn't tell what the feeling, or what the mixture of feelings, was. He almost felt cold. He felt as if someone had dumped a bucket of ice-cold water over his head while he'd been blissfully asleep, unaware of the horror which he'd experience only a moment later. It felt like the memory of the cosy slumber and the feeling of being soggy and cold. It felt like he was mourning something. It felt like he was mourning Austin.

Daniel walked to his room, not saying anything to Claire as she sat on the couch, talking to someone on the phone. He dropped into the seat beside his desk, flinging his bag to the floor. He stared at his phone, waiting for a response.

For sure! I'll get a few beers in. How do you feel about a game night?

Daniel smiled lightly to himself. He and Austin had bonded over video games when they were younger. He couldn't remember how it had happened, exactly, but they'd been working on a group project together, total strangers, when Austin had made a quippy

116

comment about a girl in the group, comparing her to a tragically awful character in a game as she'd just made a mistake which was hard to believe. Daniel had recognised the reference, laughed at it, then their relationship had simply taken off. It was the perfect example of how anything, even something miniscule, can make two people bond.

"Yeah," Daniel whispered to himself, smiling at the screen. "A game night sounds good."

Chapter 9

Daniel sat on his desk chair, staring at his phone, a smile on his face. It was the Saturday morning. He'd be visiting Austin after getting done with his classes, and he hadn't felt so excited before. He couldn't remember ever feeling so enthusiastic in his life! He was going to see a friend whom he hadn't seen in God knows how long. It had been so long that Daniel couldn't even remember what Austin looked like properly, though could vaguely remember short, curly, blonde hair which had been permed over and over to maintain the style. Austin had always looked quite sullen when he was thinking, something which Daniel had questioned him about but had found that it was nothing. Whenever he was talking to someone, too, he'd appear to be quite distant even though he was paying attention.

Daniel could remember an incident in a lesson in high school where Austin had gotten an equation wrong. The teacher had been explaining exactly what had gone wrong in as much depth as possible, only for Austin to appear as if he weren't even paying attention to the corrections. The look on his face had made the professor shout at him and send him out of the class, genuinely believing that Austin hadn't been listening, only to have been proven wrong when Austin re-entered the class and solved a very similar problem on the whiteboard, making a point of showing the entire classroom full of amused students, explaining exactly what he was doing to solve the problem. Daniel could still remember the triumphant look on Austin's face as he'd returned to his seat, the teacher stood at the side of the room, looking incredibly bashful and embarrassed.

Remembering even one thing about Austin made Daniel feel emotional, especially given that he knew what would happen the next day. He'd been thinking occasionally that, because he'd be visiting Austin the night before, maybe he'd be able to do something to stop the car accident and save Austin's life, but he didn't want to meddle too much. Daniel guessed that, as Austin had died in reality, he was destined to die even in Daniel's subconscious. Daniel didn't know a reality where Austin hadn't been killed and, even though Daniel didn't know a reality where he'd managed to get his PhD, where he hadn't been fired from his job as a waiter, where he hadn't been dating Laura throughout the last year, where he hadn't grown addicted to cigarettes, Daniel just couldn't believe that there was a chance of Austin surviving, especially given that he didn't want to get his hopes up. If he'd manage to trick himself into believing that Austin would live, if he'd end up dying anyway, Daniel would feel foolish and ashamed of hoping for a better outcome against what people would refer to as "fate."

Daniel slid his phone into his pocket and grabbed his backpack, leaving the dormitory to go to

Immunology. He only had to get through an hour and a half of Immunology, then he'd be off for one.

Getting through Immunology was a mixture of simplicity and a complicated flurry of wishing that he could just disappear from the lesson and get to Austin sooner. Daniel spent the hour and a half simply glancing at the clock whenever he had a spare moment to breathe, then following up by noting something down, trying to fixate himself on the work, only to glance up again a few minutes later with the next moment of silence within the room.

By the time that Daniel came out on the other side, all of the work done, homework set for the next lesson, only a few seconds left to go, Daniel let out a shaky sigh of relief, smiled to himself, then rushed back to his dormitory to drop off his backpack and to grab his wallet. He was going to get to Austin by bus as he didn't have a car, nor a licence at that time, for that matter, so he needed his wallet for his bus pass. It was a pity that Daniel knew how to drive in the real world, yet he didn't have a licence with him as he'd only taken his lessons after finishing university.

Daniel breezed in and out of the dormitory, barely telling Derek that he wouldn't be there for the rest of the day, maybe not until the Sunday morning. Derek barely managed to ask Daniel where he was going before Daniel closed the door again, having ignored the question.

After getting off of the campus and to the closest bus stop, Daniel waited, tapping his foot impatiently as if every tap on the ground would vibrate the earth underneath the bus and made it speed up.

It ended up taking fifteen minutes for the bus to turn up. Daniel climbed on, flashed his bus pass to the driver as if it were made of gold and he was a pimp, then flopped onto the closest seat and stared out of the window, trying to imagine what the experience would be like.

He's going to be just as I remember him, Daniel realised, happy with the thought. As he hadn't truly seen Austin since leaving for university, Daniel didn't know what he'd have *really* been like at that moment. He could have turned into an extremely unlikable person, someone whom Daniel wouldn't have been able to get along with, but Daniel wouldn't know as he'd never taken Austin up on his offer. Now, however, he *had* taken the offer and knew that his mind would almost definitely resort to just using the eighteen-year-old version of Austin instead of the twenty-two or twenty-three-year-old which he was.

Daniel stared out of the window, watching the buildings and streets whizz by. It only ended up taking around half an hour to arrive at his stop where he promptly got off and felt a wave of nostalgia. He hadn't been in that portion of the city for a long, long time. He simply never found the need to visit. There wasn't anything there which was notable except for Austin's parent's house and, as Daniel had found out over a brief text conversation the night before, Austin's tiny apartment which he'd barely managed to survive in as it was so small.

Daniel walked down the road, looking out for the building which the apartment was in. The building was supposed to be thin and tall, one right on the corner of a street and, after a moment of looking around, Daniel's eyes caught the three-storey building before he hurried across the road and towards it.

After approaching the buzzer, Daniel pressed the button for Austin's apartment, number five, and heard the annoying, loud buzz which had alerted Austin that Daniel was there.

Daniel pulled his phone out to check the time. Half-two. Not bad. He was thirty minutes early.

"Hello?" Came a deep voice from the speakers.

Daniel held the button down. "Hey, Austin! It's me."

Daniel thought he heard a small laugh of pleasure. "Brilliant! Come up, the door's unlocked."

As if Austin were magic, the door clicked, signifying that the magnets which had been holding it closed had been released. Daniel realised that thinking of the door magnificently unlocking as magic was stupid a moment later as Austin had a button in his apartment which would control the door, but given what the unlocked door would lead him to, Daniel felt as if he'd just witnessed altering reality and defying physics.

Daniel pushed the door open and rushed up the stairs to the top floor. Each floor had two apartments, the stairs in the middle of the building, making each apartment really wide and narrow due to the structure of

122

the building, something which Daniel found very slightly amusing as the thought of a living room filled up with only a couch seemed silly.

Once Daniel made it to the top floor, he stood outside of the door to Austin's apartment and took a deep breath. A couple walked out of the apartment behind him, a stroller with a baby inside in front them. They ignored Daniel as he stared at the door.

"Okay," Daniel whispered to himself, excited. He held his hand in front of him and knocked on the door twice.

The door flew open and Austin stood there, staring at Daniel with a giant, toothy grin on his face.

"It's been a while, hasn't it?" He stated stupidly, leaning forwards to give Daniel a light hug. "How long? A few years?"

Daniel shrugged lightly. "Three, I think."

"Three? It's felt like five!" Austin let out, seeming bewildered. He led Daniel into the apartment and swung the door closed behind him.

As Daniel had guessed before, the apartment was comedically laid out. It was open plan except for two doors, one which led to a bathroom, presumably, with the other leading to Austin's bedroom.

"Nice place," Daniel said nonchalantly, a grin on his face which Austin noticed.

"Don't take the piss," he said even though he also looked amused. "It's better than what you've got."

"Yeah, well, anything's better than a bedroom, a single, shared room and a shared bathroom," Daniel admitted, flopping onto the couch which was pressed up against the wall opposite to the door, barely enough space for two people to walk side-by-side in front of it.

Austin walked to the fridge and pulled it open, pulling out two beers. "Might as well get started on these now," he said, seeming unsure but willing to just go with the flow and see where they'd end up.

"As long as we don't end up more drunk than that time at the party," Daniel remarked, taking the beer from Austin, popping the seal afterwards.

Austin laughed a little. "God, yeah. Trish's birthday."

"I had to carry you home," Daniel recalled, laughing before he forced himself to stop in order to take a sip of his drink.

"That doesn't beat how Jake wasn't even aware of what was going on around him, though," Austin stated, reminding Daniel of the night. Jake and Trish had a strange rivalry and, as a dare, Trish had told him to drink five shots of vodka in a row. It didn't end well, to say the least. Jake ended up unconscious on the couch for the majority of the party, puking when he wasn't asleep, except for directly after taking the shots when, according to him, he'd blacked out, essentially, though his brain was still functioning and making his body move around and interact with people. To him, it must have been as if someone had taken control of his mind and had forced him to do different things while his conscious slept in the background.

The two of them sat for a moment, remembering

the party, the two of them amused, before Austin placed his beer on the floor and stood up to turn on a gaming console, something which sparked a sudden wave of nostalgia inside of Daniel as he and Austin hadn't played together in what felt like eons.

As Austin set everything up, Daniel couldn't help but follow the urge to pose a simple, boring question. "What's been going on with you, then?"

"Huh?" Austin replied unhelpfully, either having missed the question or not knowing what Daniel was asking.

"Since we last saw each other," Daniel said. "What's changed?"

"Not much, to be honest," Austin admitted. "I've started working in a clothing shop."

"Enjoying it?"

"Not in the slightest," Austin replied as he turned around, two controllers in his hands, laughing lightly to himself. "I've hated the place since my first day."

"Why are you still there, then?" Daniel questioned, confused. "If you hate it so much, why not get another job?"

"It pays pretty well," Austin began. He'd dropped a controller into Daniel's lap and held the other in his left hand, using his right hand to hold up fingers which stood for each point. "I'm close to a promotion, the manager's nice, it's really close to here and my shifts are good."

Daniel tilted his head to the side slightly,

considering what Austin had said. "Fair enough," he let out. "Anything else been going on?"

"Not really," Austin said with a sigh. "I've mainly been trying to keep my spending as low as possible so that I can have reliable savings."

"Fascinating."

"Shut up." Austin laughed slightly, picking his beer up and taking a sip before he placed it between his knees, squeezing them together very lightly to keep it in place while he fiddled with the controller, choosing a game for them to play. "I had a girlfriend for two months."

Daniel raised his eyebrows slightly, about to ask why it had only been a two-month-long relationship, but Austin beat him to it, elaborating.

"She had to move away," he explained. "We started dating, then she found out that her parents were moving across the country. She didn't want to be so far away from them, so she followed."

Daniel remained quiet for a moment. "Did you love her?"

"After two months, not as much as I could have," Austin admitted. "We were still getting into the relationship, really. She was shy and, you know me, I'm shy, too, so we hardly spoke unless we were forced to for the first two weeks," he recalled. "We only went on two, small dates, probably kissed a total of four times, barely even held hands."

"So, you were both acting as if you were five?"

"Pretty much," Austin agreed. "She was sweet

and pretty, but, honestly, I didn't miss her much when she left."

They quieted, the two of them focusing on the TV as Austin skipped through the opening cutscene of the game which would play before the title-screen would even appear.

"How's life for you?" Austin asked, not looking at Daniel as he asked the question, setting up a multiplayer game.

"Okay, I suppose," Daniel muttered, thinking back to what had happened in the real world. Though, something strange which he noticed was that thinking back to his feelings was surprisingly hard. He could barely remember how he'd felt when Laura had broken things off, he definitely couldn't remember the feeling of being fired over the phone as he'd already been feeling numb, and he barely even processed that his family cat had been killed on the same day, too. The sight of the motorbike rider crashing into the two, fighting pedestrians was still in his memory, though Daniel couldn't think of how to even begin picturing the sight of the man's cracked, bleeding skull. He guessed that around a month or two had passed in his long dream, and that seemed to have been long enough for him to get over the majority of what had happened. The only thing which Daniel wasn't entirely over was the fact that Laura had blatantly admitted to cheating on him and not loving him for so long. Other than that, he was more or less fine.

"Okay?" Austin questioned. "Why only

'okay?'"

"Well, university's a bit of a drag after a while," he stated. "Biochemistry's interesting and it's the field which I want to go into, but God, it's taxing."

Austin let out a small laugh which clearly had the tone of "I told you so."

"What're you laughing at?" Daniel questioned, already knowing what was coming.

"That's exactly why I didn't bother with university," Austin said. He tapped the controller in Daniel's lap, signifying for him to pick it up and set up his character. "I'm smart. I knew that university would be really, really hard, so school until eighteen was fine with me."

Daniel rolled his eyes. "And, because of that decision, you're *really* happy, aren't you?"

"Happier than you," Austin corrected. The two of them went silent for a moment while the game began loading.

"I'm going to kick your arse, Danny."

Daniel snickered slightly. "Bring it on," he challenged.

The two of them ended up staying like that, sat on the couch, playing a handful of video games, watching a film at one point, talking with each other, joking around, catching-up and drinking a few beers for what felt like only an hour. In reality, however, seven hours passed, the two of them looking up at the clock on the wall simultaneously to see that it was almost ten in the evening.

"Time sure flies when you're having fun," Austin stated, laughing at the cheesiness of the claim.

"Yeah," Daniel agreed, slightly meek. He knew that it was time to go, but he didn't want to. Austin was due to die the next day. But, maybe, there was a chance that he could change that. He could remember that, according to the phone-call from Austin's mother, the crash had happened in the morning while Austin was going on a run. Maybe he could postpone Austin's schedule? "Do you have a shift tomorrow?"

Austin looked at Daniel for a second, contemplating. "Yeah, in the afternoon," he said after a moment of trying to remember. "Why?"

"Just curious," Daniel said, looking away and around at the room, searching for inspiration. "I was just wondering if it would do any harm for me to stay a little longer."

"Midnight's good for me," Austin said, shrugging. "I'm fine with staying up until then. I'm fine to be in bed until eleven in the morning, anyway."

Daniel nodded lightly, happy with that. At the very least, if he couldn't stop Austin from dying, he could spend a little more time with him.

"Cool," Daniel said, a small grin on his face.

"I'll get us some more beer," Austin said, picking up the two empty cans from the floor and taking them to the kitchen.

"I'll just head to the bathroom," Daniel stated, placing the controller on the seat as he stood up. He walked past Austin and purposefully walked through the

129

wrong door, heading into Austin's bedroom. Austin didn't even seem to notice.

Once inside, Daniel strained his eyes in the dark, but eventually caught sight of Austin's alarm clock. He made sure to tip-toe towards it, following the dull, red light which emanated from the numbers on the screen. Then, when close enough, he reached out and pressed the button to see when the alarm was set. Eight in the morning. No good.

Daniel pressed a button to disable the alarm, hoping that Austin wouldn't check to make sure that it was working before going to bed. Well, hopefully, he wouldn't if Daniel would be able to tire him out enough before leaving. That seemed like the only way to properly postpone Austin's death or, ideally, prevent it completely.

Daniel left Austin's bedroom, then walked through the open door to the bathroom, holding the door closed before he flushed the toilet, waited for a few moments, then walked out of the room. Austin hadn't noticed a single thing.

"Done," Daniel said, heading back to the couch. He took his already-opened beer from Austin, then took a sip, feeling satisfied and hopeful that his plan would render some results.

"Another game?" Austin inquired, placing his beer on the floor, holding his controller up.

"Sounds good," Daniel stated, nodding slightly.

By the time that it was midnight, Daniel could tell that Austin was tired. He wasn't sure just how tired his friend was, but hoped that it was enough.

"I'd better be off now, then," Daniel stated, standing up a few moments after they'd just finished another game. "I have work tomorrow, too."

Austin gave a small nod, then stood up and walked to the door with Daniel.

"It's been great to see you again," he said, pulling Daniel in for a hug.

They remained in the embrace for a few moments before Daniel decided to pull away. He flashed a coy smile at Austin, then took a step backwards and out of the door.

"See you soon, hopefully," Daniel said, taking a moment to look at his friend before he turned and walked away, heading down the stairs, hoping that his plan would prevent a catastrophe.

Chapter 10

It was the following Saturday and Daniel was sat in Immunology, trying to distract himself from the thought of his and Elisha's upcoming date. He felt uncomfortable being sat there, pondering what would happen. He was excited. He wanted to just get to what was going to happen. He hadn't been on a date in a long, long time, so it was an exciting prospect: going on one with someone whom he hadn't dated before.

Daniel tried to distract himself from his thoughts with the work which was in front of him.

He hadn't heard anything about Austin so, hopefully, that meant that he was okay. After Daniel had gotten back home a little less than a week before, he'd thrown himself into his bed and had ended up crying, thinking about his and Austin's friendship, scared that he'd end up dying again. Even though it wasn't real life, Daniel had felt as if he'd regained his friend by seeing him again. He didn't want to have Austin back for such a short amount of time and then lose him again. That was the last thing which he wanted.

The rest of the week had been slow. Daniel hadn't spoken very much with Bryan, Claire nor Derek. Bryan had an upcoming exam, Derek was bombarded with homework, and Claire was worn out from a combination of school-life and relationship-life. Apparently, that boy whom she'd met at Henry's party had evolved from being a one-time occurrence to a much more prominent person in Claire's life. She'd decided to keep the whole thing as much of a secret as possible, but she hadn't succeeded for very long as she'd ended up having a breakdown in front of Bryan after having been dumped. Bryan had promptly informed Daniel and Derek about what was going on and, after stopping Derek from paying the boy a visit, Claire had told them that she just wanted some time to deal with it all. Therefore, she hadn't stepped outside of her bedroom when it was possible.

Daniel and Elisha hadn't talked very much, either. They'd decided on what they'd be doing for their date, however: having dinner in a restaurant, then returning to Daniel's dorm to spend some time together and to do whatever they'd fancy when the time would come. Elisha had been the one to decide on going back to Daniel's dorm and, even though it made Daniel slightly nervous as the last time that they'd been alone and in his dormitory, they'd been discussing their relationship and, of course, the time before that hadn't exactly been keeping it to cuddling on the couch, he was fine with the idea.

Daniel looked over towards Elisha. She had her head down, writing, focusing on her work, but Daniel could almost tell just from looking at the side of her head that she was slightly distracted. Her lips were pressed together as if she was struggling to keep herself from doing something, focusing on the squeezing feeling as much as possible to distract herself. Her left leg was bouncing up and down to a somewhat fast tempo, and her left hand would occasionally flick up slightly before landing back on the table. It was as if she was drumming to keep herself focused.

Daniel found that the rest of the lesson progressed in a similar fashion. Then, once it had finally ended, he and Elisha alongside everyone else began heading back to their dormitories, their lesson for the day having been completed.

Daniel ended up returning to his dormitory and, after giving a quick "hello" to Bryan as he sat on the couch, reading through notes, he retreated to his room.

He and Elisha had decided that their date would take place at seven in the evening, giving Daniel a lot of time to kill. It was only twenty-to-two.

After a small amount of consideration, Daniel decided that it would be best to simply get as much homework done as possible. If he could clear out a decent chunk of the work on his desk and on his computer, he'd be able to have a much more relaxed mind over the following days. Being more relaxed would definitely be beneficial if there was any chance of his and Elisha's date leading to anything more in the future. It wouldn't be good for the two of them to end up lovestruck and unable to focus on getting their important work done.

Daniel ended up sitting at his desk for a little more than two hours, getting as much of his homework done as he could manage. By the time that he finally decided to take a break, it was almost four in the afternoon.

"Three hours left," Daniel muttered to himself, leaning back in his chair. He'd just completed an essay for Virology, leaving only two pieces of homework for Biochemistry and a single piece of homework for Immunology. That was substantially better than the six assignments which he'd had before he'd started working.

Daniel stood up and went to the bathroom, using it before heading to the kitchen for a drink of water. Bryan was still sat on the couch, notes in hand, looking extremely stressed. "Why don't you take a break for a bit?" Daniel suggested.

Bryan looked up and considered the thought. "Okay," he said, placing the papers onto the coffee table. "For half an hour."

"It looks like you might need longer than that, to be honest," Daniel informed him, taking a long gulp of the water contained in the glass in his hands before placing the empty tumbler into the sink. "You look like a zombie."

Bryan smirked a little. "Forty-five minutes, then," he said, leaning back into the couch. He suddenly looked much more relaxed as if he'd been sitting and waiting for someone to tell him to take a break. Daniel hoped that wasn't the case as he'd done something similar in the past, vowing to himself that he wouldn't stop revising until someone would tell him to stop. It had ended up taking four and a half hours before Derek had dragged the papers away from him, had given him some snacks and a beer and had forced him to sit and watch a film with him and Claire.

"Good," Daniel said, smirking a little. He flopped onto the couch beside Bryan.

"When's your date with Elisha?" Bryan asked, moving his head only a little to look at Daniel as if he had limited movement in his neck.

"At seven," Daniel stated. "I'd better start getting ready at six."

"What're you going to do?" Bryan questioned.

"Dinner, then we'll come back here."

Bryan gave a nod which made him look as if he was a very important person at a company. "Okay, I'll make sure that we're all out of your way."

Daniel raised his eyebrows slightly. "You don't *have* to stay away," he said. "We're all friends, so…"

"Yeah, but will you make out with her if we're in the room?" Bryan interjected, turning to properly look at Daniel. He looked smug.

"I won't regardless," Daniel muttered though, in all honesty, he wasn't completely certain.

Bryan turned to look at the blank screen of the TV. "You never know," he simply stated, looking too confident with the idea that something would happen between Daniel and Elisha.

"Whatever you say," Daniel said, slightly amused by Bryan's insistence but also slightly embarrassed.

136

The two of them stayed together for the remainder of Bryan's break, moving to play a game until Bryan decided that it was time to get back to work. Once he'd decided as such, Daniel decided to retreat to his room again to spend some time on his computer. Afterwards, at around six, he decided to get ready, taking a shower, shaving, then getting into some of the smartest-yet-casual clothes which he had. After that, Daniel simply sat on his bed, watching the clock. Would it hurt to text Elisha?

I'm ready when you are. Come to my dorm when you're ready to go.

Daniel put his phone down for a moment, staring around his room, bored but unwilling to risk getting himself roped into an activity out of fear of being late.

His phone buzzed, and after checking it, Daniel saw that Elisha had replied.

I'll be there in ten.

Daniel let out a small, content sigh, then stepped out of his room and into the main living area.

Bryan had left, presumably having gone into his room to either continue studying or to spend some time on his own. Claire was on the couch, now, watching something on the TV.

"When will she be here?" Claire asked, not taking her eyes away from the show.

"Ten minutes or so," Daniel informed, ignoring the grinning reflection of Claire on the screen.

"We'll make sure to stay out of your way when you come back here," she assured. "But I can't promise that we won't watch."

"Really?" Daniel asked, unamused. "Even if we have-"

"God, no!" Claire let out, laughing afterwards. "We'll stop if that happens, I promise."

They went quiet. Daniel stood behind the couch, leaning on the back of it, watching the show alongside Claire until a knock came from the door.

Daniel headed to the door and pulled it open, revealing Elisha. She looked absolutely stunning. She was also dressed fairly casually, in a white crop-top, a dark, blue cardigan and black leggings, her black hair having been clearly washed at least three times, appearing silky-smooth and slightly shiny due to the hairspray which she'd used. She only had a small amount of make-up on, a small amount of eyeshadow and eyeliner along with a tinge of blush. Daniel couldn't look away from her.

"Hey," she said with a slightly high-pitched voice. She flashed a sweet smile.

"Um, hello," Daniel replied, returning the smile with a nervous one. "Ready to go?"

"…Yeah."

"You two don't need to be so damn awkward!" Claire called to them, staring at them via their reflections in the strip of glossy plastic which outlined the TV.

Daniel and Elisha laughed, the two of them acknowledging what Claire had said, realising that it was stupid to be embarrassed. Daniel knew that he'd

138

been excited about the date since it had been arranged. Nervous, true, but still excited. Why waste time being awkward?

Elisha stepped back, giving Daniel enough room to leave the dormitory.

"Don't get back too late!" Claire called.

"Yes, mum!" Daniel replied, amused. He closed the door, listening to Elisha's suppressed giggling.

"Right," she began, turning to walk away before she paused and, after a moment of hesitation, held her hand out towards Daniel, then pulled it back after a second, deciding against holding his hand.

Daniel watched her, confused and amused, before he simply snatched her left hand with his right and clutched it loosely. "Come on," he said, beginning to walk.

Elisha strolled beside him, the two of them heading down the hallway, arriving at the stairs, carefully walking down those as Elisha had decided that, even though she didn't have the best balance while walking in them, she was going to wear slightly elevated platforms.

Once they'd made it off of the campus, they began walking in the direction of the restaurant.

Daniel had booked a table a few nights before, not wanting there to be any chance of them turning up and finding the place completely filled up. It *was* a Saturday night, after all, so there were almost definitely going to be a slurry of other people filling up the establishment, and Daniel didn't fancy wandering around the city in search of somewhere which wasn't packed with people. The table which Daniel had reserved had been booked for five-past-seven given that the restaurant wasn't very far away from the university campus.

Daniel pulled his phone out of his pocket with his left hand, checking the time. They had five minutes to get there. That was plenty of time.

The two of them continued their stroll, walking slightly slowly, enjoying the fresh, cool air. Daniel almost felt as if he was in a real dream, not a lucid one which he was aware of, and snapped out of his stupor after a moment, confused and surprised.

"The sky's pretty," Elisha stated after a moment, craning her neck slightly to look up at the sky, her head at a slightly unflattering angle.

"Yeah," Daniel replied after having glanced up at it. The moon was barely visible behind a few, lonesome clouds. It must have been the only cluster of clouds in the sky, though Daniel couldn't see through the buildings which obscured some of his vision to check if that was correct. The stars were twinkling very slightly but, being someone studying for a PhD which was heavily, *heavily* related to science, Daniel only wondered just how many of those stars were actually dead already, having died long, long ago, yet their light was only just reaching Earth, a constant, lengthy beam of solar power which had been aimed at their planet, shooting through the galaxy like a bullet from a gun which had fired its last round.

The walk continued for another minute until they came across the restaurant, catching sight of it across a road. They crossed and stood outside of it, confirming that it was the correct place before they stepped inside.

A woman greeted them, waiting for a moment until Daniel gave his name. She checked a computer, found a table for them, then led them over to it. It was small and secluded, fairly far away from the more populated areas of the restaurant and, Daniel noticed, it was quieter than he'd initially expected. Whenever he'd thought of the population of the restaurant, he'd simply assumed that, as it was a Saturday, it was going to be bustling yet, surprisingly, it was fairly calm. It wasn't close to empty, but there was a significantly smaller percentage of people inside.

The two of them sat down, were given menus, then were left alone.

"It's nice in here," Elisha stated with a calm, almost bouncy voice. She eyed-up the room, looking at the beams on the ceiling, the slightly slanted and painted stone walls, the refurbished and stylish floorboards and the feature wall to her left and Daniel's right, painted red to contrast with the modern-looking light-grey colour of the other walls.

"It is," Daniel agreed, slightly impressed and hopeful. The sight of an emptier-than-usual establishment on such a busy night was slightly unsettling but, seeing as the place looked clean and taken care of, Daniel doubted that there'd be any need to worry about the quality of the food.

After a few moments of looking at their menus, a waitress came over, requesting their drink orders. Elisha decided on a red wine, Merlot, while Daniel decided that, given what had happened between them the last time that they'd gotten drunk, he didn't want to have to go through another, awkward morning, ordering a non-alcoholic red wine, hoping that it wouldn't taste disgusting as he'd never tried one before yet didn't want to have a glass of water with his dinner.

The waitress took their orders, left, then, after a few moments, Elisha posed a question. "Not scared of getting drunk with me again, are you?" She asked rhetorically, jokingly, yet there also seemed to be a slight tinge of concern within her tone.

"Not really," Daniel stated, lying. "Just had a lot of alcohol recently."

Elisha snickered lightly, then quieted, paying attention to the menu laying on the table in front of her. She spent a moment thinking, then decided, not saying what she wanted out-loud, simply closing the menu and sliding it away from herself and towards the centre of the table. Daniel copied her, deciding what he wanted after a moment before he stacked his menu on top of Elisha's.

"So, let's just get right to it, huh?" Elisha suggested, leaning forwards, looking at Daniel with a slight eagerness in her eyes. "I'm just going to be honest with you."

"Okay?"

"Don't let it make things awkward if you don't feel the same way."

Daniel stared at her, contemplating what was going to happen. It was clear that Elisha was planning to tell him exactly how she felt whether she liked him or not. Daniel could tell that she was about to be honest with him and, in a weird way, that made him both excited and terrified. *He* didn't even know how *he* felt!

"Daniel, I-"

"Don't," Daniel interjected, holding his hand in front of her face softly. "Not yet."

Elisha leaned back in her seat and stared at him, looking interested. "Why?" She questioned. "Still trying to figure it all out?"

Daniel gave a light, almost shy nod. "Yeah," he admitted. "This date is for, well, figuring it all out, right?"

Elisha considered his words, remaining silent, watching him with as much eagerness and interest as a lion would watch a zebra.

"You might end up changing your mind about it all over the next two or three hours," Daniel continued, leaning back as well, almost as if he was trying to get as far away from the predator which was hunting his feelings as possible. "You never know."

Elisha let out a small breath which Daniel almost mistook for a sigh. She leaned back into the table, her arms resting, crossed on the tablecloth. "Okay," she said, then smiled. "Good point."

Daniel let out a small breath, relieved. He leaned

in, too, making it seem to onlookers as if they were both in love and enjoying a romantic date when, in reality, Daniel, at least, was still trying to figure out if there *was* any love.

The waitress returned with their drinks after a moment, placing the respective drink in front of who ordered it before she asked for what they'd be eating. Steak for both of them, exactly as presented on the menu, medium-rare. Daniel almost laughed at how similar they were. They were both having the exact same meal and their drinks were the same barring the fact that Daniel's glass of wine didn't even contain a spec of alcohol. He wondered if they were both unconsciously copying each other or it was all a strange coincidence.

They talked for a while about random things, doing their best to try to figure out if they truly *liked* the other person, trying to see if there were any hints that the other liked them or not, trying to find *anything* to talk about to pass the time. There wasn't much to discover about the other person given that they'd already had a long conversation regarding themselves, so they largely ended up resorting to either hunting for new pieces of information to share or to chatting about what had happened over the past few days. At one point, they even managed to get into discussing their PhDs, something which they pulled away from once they'd realised what had happened as they didn't want to discuss their school-life while on a date.

Their food arrived after twenty minutes of

waiting and, after eating it fairly quickly and very slightly unromantically, they both decided to skip out on desserts, something which Daniel was secretly glad for as he didn't have much money even after saving as much as possible from his part-time job. Something which was pleasant, however, was that Elisha decided that she was going to pay for both of them. She didn't accept any compromises of them splitting the cheque, she didn't even want Daniel to simply chip in, even with a small amount. She paid the entire bill and promised Daniel, quite cheekily and playfully, he thought, that he owed her something in the future, though made sure not to disclose exactly what she had in mind. Daniel guessed that it was going to end up being a free ticket to seeing him doing something dumb, and, even if that was the case, he wasn't going to object.

They left the restaurant and began heading back to the campus. For a small amount of time, they were silent, simply enjoying each other's company, taking a few moments occasionally to comment on what was going on around them. They heard a shout in the distance at one point and theorised about what the reason for the noise was, they saw someone sprinting down the road, not looking as if he was going on an evening jog, and they heard a flurry of police sirens not too far from them, making the two of them slightly excited as they wondered what had happened.

By the time that they'd arrived back on the campus and were walking up the stairs to Daniel's floor, it was twenty-to-eight in the evening.

They emerged onto Daniel's floor and trotted towards his dormitory, pushing the door open to see that the others had either retreated from the main area or that they weren't home.

"Want a beer?" Daniel asked, then paused and looked at Elisha. "Or would that be a bad idea?"

Elisha rolled her eyes slightly, then moved to the couch and sat down. "I'm okay," she said, watching Daniel as he walked to the couch and sat next to her.

The two of them were silent for a moment, Daniel feeling slightly awkward as he had vivid memories of the embarrassment which he'd felt the last time when Elisha had been there with him, then the knowledge of what had happened the time before that. Though, at least, he was completely sober, so it wasn't likely that anything was going to escalate.

"I'll be blunt Daniel, I like you," Elisha let out after a moment, catching Daniel completely off-guard.

"Wha- Oh! Right, I see," he spluttered. "I-I mean, yeah, me, too. No, not that I like me, but that- you know, right?"

Elisha stared at him, amused by how bashful he was being. She reached out and placed a finger on his top lip, telling him to be quiet. "I know what you mean," she muttered, smiling. "You like me, too, right?"

Daniel nodded very slightly. "Yeah," he whispered, relieved that Elisha had said the words for him. "Is that… okay?"

She raised her eyebrows as she pulled her finger away from Daniel's mouth. "Okay?" She repeated.

"Duh! Of course it's okay!"

She leaned forwards and gave him a hug.

Daniel held her, relieved. Over the course of their date, he'd realised that the excitement which he'd felt regarding the event had to have meant *something*. Why would he be excited for a date with someone whom he didn't feel attracted to? Daniel knew that it meant that he, at the very least, liked Elisha somewhat, though he'd wanted to get through their dinner to see if the feelings were true. Daniel had found that he couldn't properly keep his eyes off of her, that he was consistently interested as to what she was saying, finely tuned into the conversation like an old radio having been set by a robot. He was interested in her, at least, but Daniel had the feeling that it was more than just liking the idea of dating her, that it was more than just being curious as to what it would be like. He could say, with at least some certainty, that he liked her.

Elisha pulled away from him. "Remind me to never ask you anything important like that again," she joked, laughing silently, her mouth slightly open as she moved back and forth slightly, her eyes showing her amusement.

"Could you kiss me?" Daniel asked suddenly, his voice as calm as he could make it.

Elisha looked at him, eyebrows raised, before she nodded very slightly and leaned in, giving him a quick kiss on the lips before she pulled away and gave a smile which clearly asked him if that was okay.

"You know, I remember that feeling," she said

147

after a moment, laughing, clearly embarrassed. Daniel felt embarrassed, too, knowing what she was referring to, but he was just happy that she didn't seem to be revolted by him.

"So, what do you want to do, then?" Daniel asked her.

"I don't know, it's up to you-"

"No, I mean about us."

Elisha looked at him, pondering something. "I'll date you if you'll date me."

Daniel smiled and nodded enthusiastically. "Yeah!" He let out, happy with the idea of the two of them being together. "Let's date, then."

The two of them spent the rest of their time together watching a film, trying their best not to be awkward about their new relationship status. They weren't staying away from each other as if scared that the other was carrying a deadly disease, but they weren't exactly lovey-dovey, either. Elisha barely had the courage to make the first move after their initial flow of moving forwards had ended, leaning into Daniel slightly and taking his hand after twenty minutes of sitting apart from each other. From there, it didn't escalate very much. Daniel hadn't been trying to count, but, by the end of the film, he realised that they'd kissed each other a total of four times over the two hours that they'd been there, pressed against each other slightly. He didn't mind a slower start but could remember that Laura definitely hadn't held back after they'd just gotten together.

"I'd better get going," Elisha said once the film had ended, having just held onto Daniel for a few minutes after requesting to just sit in silence with each other for a small while, wanting to simply enjoy the company which they had.

Daniel nodded lightly, more confident than he'd previously been. "Okay," he said, standing up. He pulled Elisha from the couch and walked her to the door, feeling slightly strange doing so as, the last time which they'd done it had been only week-or-so before and, as far as he'd known then, he hadn't felt an ounce of attraction towards Elisha.

"I'll text you tomorrow," Elisha said, stepping out of the door. She turned around to look at Daniel, giving him a sweet, cute smile.

"Yeah," Daniel said, returning the smile.

Elisha stepped forwards and gave Daniel a quick kiss and a hug before pulling away and beginning to walk towards the stairs.

Daniel watched Elisha walk down the hallway for a few moments before he closed the door and began leaning against it. Thinking about Laura a moment before, even though it had been an extremely brief comparison, just gave Daniel a small wave of fear. He knew that he was over or, at least, mostly over Laura, but that didn't mean that he wasn't scared that something like that could happen again. He could tell that he'd genuinely started to think of Elisha as a girl whom he really, really liked at the very least, so thinking about the possibility of her... No, she wouldn't. But, even so…

"No," Daniel whispered to himself, adamant that Elisha wouldn't anything *nearly* as cruel as Laura. Elisha wasn't that type of girl, and he could tell that. Yet, even so, that didn't stop the fear from being present in his mind.

It'll be better than my last relationship, Daniel told himself. *I can promise myself that, at least.*

Chapter 11

Daniel sat up in his bed, tired. He'd been emailed the day before to request for him to go into work for an extra shift that Sunday, combining his already-existing one with the new one to provide a five-hour-long shift starting from eleven in the morning. Usually, that wouldn't have bothered Daniel so much, but he'd only been emailed the night before at one in the morning after having spent a long time catching up with an unfair amount of homework due for Virology.

After silencing his alarm, Daniel let out a long yawn before clambering out from under his duvet. It was only nine in the morning, but he was exhausted. He must have been working for at least three hours straight the previous night, and that had come after a long day, regardless. He'd had a stressful school day, then had spent a fair amount of time with Elisha, Derek and Claire while Bryan had been catching up with homework of his own. He and Elisha had agreed that they didn't have to get the homework done for a little bit of time, that they'd be able to get through it over the Sunday, but Daniel had decided to jump the gun after returning to his room. That, while it had technically been a brilliant idea as he wouldn't have had as long to work on it with his extended shift, left Daniel too exhausted. Even *thinking* about the shift which he'd be leaving for within two hours was enough to ware him out all over again.

Daniel opened his wardrobe and pulled his uniform out, carrying it with him and through the living area, heading to the bathroom for a shower. He laid the uniform on the lid of the toilet before he turned the shower on, turned to the sink to brush his teeth while waiting for the water to heat up, then undressed completely and climbed into the shower.

The shower was quick, only a few minutes, then Daniel climbed out and got dressed, pulling everything on with care, not wanting to scuff the clothes or to crease them in a way which would make him look unprofessional and messy.

Daniel looked at himself in the mirror, making sure that he looked presentable, then gave himself a light, affirmative nod before leaving the bathroom.

"What's with the clothes?" Derek asked, turning around to look at him, a joke at the ready. "Wedding? Funeral?"

"Work," Daniel stated, rolling his eyes a little. He walked to the kitchen area and started to make a bowl of cereal for breakfast, then grabbed a glass of orange juice and downed it within a few moments, proceeding to pick up the bowl of cereal and take it to the couch, watching the TV as Derek tried to play a notoriously difficult game.

"You look shattered," Derek stated, not pulling his eyes away from the screen at all as he'd come across a particularly challenging part of the game.

"I am," Daniel stated, putting a spoonful of cereal into his mouth. He swallowed it quickly before elaborating slightly. "Worked for three hours last night."

"Finished it?"

"Just about," Daniel confirmed. "I need to write another paragraph or two, so I'll do that later."

"Or you could just get it done while you wait to leave…" Derek stated, his voice trailing off as his focus turned to the game entirely.

Daniel considered that, then decided that it was a better idea than just waiting around. He wouldn't have so much stress if he'd do that, at least. He could get the work done, get through his lengthened shift, then sleep for the rest of the day if he wanted.

After finishing his breakfast, Daniel returned to his room, taking half-an-hour to finish the essay before he spent twenty minutes reading over the entirety of the script, correcting small mistakes, adding bits and pieces occasionally. Eventually, he finished, checking the time to see that it was a little past ten. Fifty minutes of time to relax, then he'd have to leave for work.

Daniel sent the essay to his Virology professor via email, then leaned back in his chair, letting out a deep sigh. He wanted to just retreat to bed. He'd done work, why couldn't he just leave it there?

The proceeding fifty minutes which Daniel fought through were spent with Derek and Claire, him and Claire watching Derek play, doing their best to guide him through the portion of the game even though neither of them had played it before, resulting in a few moments where the three of them had no idea what to do. At one point, Derek managed to get stuck in a death-loop, dying, respawning, trying again before dying again. It was a constant cycle before the three of them banded together to come up with a strategy which, on the third attempt, finally worked.

When the time came for Daniel to leave for his shift, he simply bid farewell to Derek and Claire while they jokingly wished him luck as if he were leaving for war. He left the dormitory and began walking down the hallway, taking a few deep breaths with hope that extra oxygen would help to wake him up and provide him with enough energy to get through five hours of rushing around, trying to help people with whatever they'd need, dealing with the imminent few people who'd feel as if they were entitled to everything just for existing. The usual shift wouldn't have been too bad given that it would have come after lunch, would have only been for two-to-three hours and, as it would have come after lunch, would have been much quieter than what he was heading towards.

Daniel descended the stairs, made his way off of the campus, then started heading towards the restaurant which he worked in. He knew that it wasn't going to take long to get there, yet he hoped that the fresh oxygen would be enough to wake him up a decent amount more than the previous deep breaths had. A five-or-less minute-long walk would help him to wake up more, right? Daniel hoped so.

Looking around as he walked, Daniel began wondering just what the shift would look like. Going in for much longer than usual felt incredibly strange, almost as if he was heading towards a completely different job. He'd never gotten through an extra shift in that restaurant in his life, mainly because he'd always be busy whenever a request would come. Daniel guessed that avoiding extra shifts was one of the reasons why he'd never received a promotion, though he hadn't expected to get one at any point, so that didn't bother him too much. A downside to how his work-life had previously been, however, was that he didn't know what to expect in terms of how bustling the restaurant would be. He had no idea if he was going to end up battling to get through the shift or if it was going to be just like every other shift which he'd had.

It took three minutes for Daniel to arrive at the restaurant. His idea of using the fresh oxygen to help him to wake up definitely worked at least somewhat, but he couldn't feel much of a change. If anything, Daniel felt practically the same barring the very, very slight difference.

Daniel stepped into the slightly busy restaurant and walked to the manager's office to check-in. Dale greeted him as soon as he opened the door, then gave him his supplies and sent Daniel on his way, telling him that he'd be working for an hour, then getting a fifteen-minute-long break.

Daniel left the office and headed to his section,

trying to prepare himself mentally for what was about to inevitably come.

After wandering around in his sector for only a few moments, Daniel was called over to a table. Just from looking over, he gathered the feeling that the ordering process was going to be unnecessarily difficult.

"Hello, sweetie," an older woman said to greet Daniel as he approached. "We're ready to order."

"Brilliant," Daniel let out, practically monotone, only a thin vail of enthusiasm to mask his tiredness. He opened his notepad and held his pen to the paper, looking between the woman and another elderly lady, the two of them probably friends having lunch together.

"Brilliant?" The woman's friend asked, raising her barely visible, grey eyebrows slightly, a few of the clearly well-taken-care-of curls of her still-brown hair bouncing slightly as she leaned back. "You don't need to sound so bored."

"I-I just-" Daniel stopped himself from replying, knowing not to fall into the hole of being ferociously devoured by old ladies searching for any reason to have their meals for free. If he'd end up upsetting them somehow, they'd probably complain to someone and demand for refunds. Daniel had dealt with people like that before, way too many than what would have seemed normal to him. He knew not to fall into their trap. "What can I get you?" He asked the woman who'd called him over.

"I'd like the Caesar salad without any cheese, an extra raw egg, double the amount of lettuce, only a few

156

drops of Worcester sauce, at least fifteen croutons because I can never seem to find *any* when I eat here, and a sprinkle of dressing."

Daniel wrote as fast as he could, trying to note down every single detail of the order, hoping that it was correct before he'd recite it back to the woman. He knew that getting anything wrong would probably just aggravate her even more than how aggravated the chefs would be to have to prepare a traditional meal with so many changes which, Daniel reckoned, made the entire salad sound like anything *other* than a Caesar salad.

"So, you'd like a Caesar salad without the parmesan cheese, with an extra raw egg, with double the lettuce, a few drops of Worcester sauce, fifteen croutons and a sprinkle of dressing?" He recited, watching the woman as he spoke, trying to look pleasant even though he felt as if he could smack her over the head with the notepad.

"Correct," the woman confirmed, flashing a sweet yet emotionless smile at him.

"What about the chicken included with the salad?" Daniel questioned, realising his mistake of asking anything else after he'd already spoken.

"If I wanted chicken, I'd have mentioned it," the woman practically spat, proving that the smile from earlier had clearly been empty.

"And, what about you?" Daniel asked, trying to hide his annoyance as he jotted down that the woman didn't want chicken, either, while turning to the lady with the perfect, brown curls.

"I'd like a Greek salad with extra spinach and extra Greek olives," the woman informed Daniel, pleasantly surprising him as he hadn't expected the order to be so straight forward.

"What would you two like to drink?" He questioned, looking between the two of them.

"Water," the brown-haired one stated flatly.

"Red wine," the other said.

"Um, I'm sorry, Ma'am, but we don't serve alcohol until it's past five in the afternoon," Daniel told her, bracing for the inevitable earthquake which would ensue.

"Really?" She asked, staring at him, looking surprisingly menacing for an old lady. "Well, you can tell whoever made that rule to-"

"The rule's in place for a reason," Daniel cut across, not wanting to end up getting into an argument with the woman and causing a big scene. He could already sense that a few people were occasionally glancing at the bratty woman, amused or surprised.

The woman silenced herself with her lips pressed so tightly together that Daniel almost expected her face to turn red from the pressure. "Fine," she let out gruffly. "Water, too."

Daniel quickly noted the drinks down, then retreated, rushing to the kitchen to give the chefs the page which had the notes on it.

Once Daniel reached the opening to the kitchen, he placed the note on the counter and, when he caught the Sous-chef's eye, mouthed an apology, gesturing to

158

the note with his eyes. The Sous-chef understood what Daniel meant immediately and let out a small sigh, moving to pick up the note. As soon as she even glanced at it, her face dropped slightly before she turned around and called the order out to everyone in the kitchen. Daniel could hear her repeating the order twice before he was called to another table.

As Daniel walked over, he saw that it was a man on his own, maybe only twenty or so, dressed-up, looking smart. He must have been on his way to or from a job interview.

"Hi, what can I get you?" Daniel asked him after stopping next to the table. His tone was much more enthusiastic than it had been while he'd been talking to the older women.

"I'll just have the French onion soup," the man said, looking pleasant.

Daniel noted it down. "What about a drink?"

"No drink, thanks," the man said. "I don't know if I could manage a drink, too. I'm a bit nervous."

"Job interview?" Daniel asked, closing the notepad though holding the page with the tip of his thumb.

"Yeah, how did you know?"

Daniel shrugged. "Just a lucky guess. Is that all?"

The man nodded lightly with a smile before Daniel turned and walked straight to the kitchen, handing the order over, surprised when he was almost immediately handed a bowl of French onion soup as a larger batch had just been finished.

Daniel carried the soup back to the man who, like Daniel, was surprised by how fast the process had been.

"Good luck with your interview," Daniel said after having placed the soup on the table in front of the man.

"Thanks. And good luck with dealing with people like that," the man replied, laughing a little. He subtly nodded towards the old woman a few tables away, smirking slightly.

Daniel grinned, then turned and walked away. It was a shame that not every customer was as pleasant as that man but, Daniel knew, that was the thing with any sort of retail where the customers would have direct contact with the business. There were always going to be at least a few people who wouldn't be as straightforward as everybody else.

The rest of Daniel's lengthened shift passed with a mixture of pleasant people and a sprinkling of bratty, entitled individuals. All in all, the shift wasn't as bad as Daniel had initially expected, though it wasn't exactly spectacular. He'd had three fifteen-minute-long breaks throughout the day, and each of them had been filled with a mixture of relief and stress as he knew that he'd be returning to the possible hellhole.

By the time that Daniel had finished serving a table and the restaurant had died down a decent amount, only five minutes to go before the end of Daniel's shift, Dale came out and motioned for Daniel to follow him.

Slightly scared that he'd done something wrong, Daniel obliged.

"What's up?" Daniel asked as they walked into Dale's office, closing the door lightly behind him while Dale walked to his desk and sat down.

"I'm going to be blunt," Dale began. "You've been terrific over the past few shifts."

"Only the past few?" Daniel joked, laughing slightly, hoping that it would put his mind to ease. Numerous possibilities were buzzing through his head. Was he going to be scolded? Was it just a check-in to see how he was coping? Was there going to be a new employee whom he'd have to train? Was he going to receive a promotion? Was he going to be fired?

Dale chuckled at Daniel's sarcasm. "Well, everyone's impressed with how you're doing," he continued. "The chefs seem to think that you've done something like this before."

"I... haven't," Daniel lied, not knowing what else to say. Was the meeting just because his co-workers were thinking of him as a natural?

Dale shrugged lightly, his shoulders barely moving. He looked slightly smug, his eyes almost closed as he stared at his desk. Dale looked up at Daniel.

"We're all very impressed, and we've all agreed that, even though you've only been here for a short while, you deserve a promotion."

"A promotion?" Daniel repeated, all worry fleeing from his mind as he stared at Dale in shock. "Really?"

Dale looked entertained. "Yes, really," he laughed. "We're looking to maybe expand and open a second restaurant somewhere else in the city, and if we're going to do that, we're going to need as many waiter trainers as possible," he explained. "In short, we'll need you to be qualified to train the waiters whom we employ in the future."

Daniel smiled to himself, satisfied. He hadn't expected a promotion. All of the changes which he'd been making to his life had worked out so well. He'd been able to keep on top of his work and, hopefully, get to a point where he'd have a decent chance of earning his PhD. He hadn't returned to smoking when he'd been offered the chance. He hadn't let himself be a pushover to the people whom he cared about the most. He hadn't skipped out on seeing Austin and, as a result, hadn't heard anything about a tragedy. He hadn't worsened his relationship with his friends out of anger due to having missed his last chance to see Austin. And, finally, he hadn't ruined his chances of keeping a job which he genuinely enjoyed. He was getting a promotion!

"What do you think about that, then?" Dale asked, leaning forwards on his desk, his elbows upright with his chin resting on his bent hands.

"I'd be more than happy to take the responsibility," Daniel stated after a moment with an affirmative nod.

Dale smiled lightly before standing up and heading over to Daniel. He grabbed Daniel's hand and gave him a firm handshake. "Brilliant!" He let out, patting Daniel on the side of his right arm with his left hand. "Now, your wage will be increasing slightly, you'll have to be trained to train other waiters, but you won't have any extra shifts than you do now," Dale explained.

Daniel nodded slightly as he listened to Dale, like a student being told how to solve an equation.

Once Dale had finished his brief explanation which detailed just what the training which Daniel would be receiving would entail, he dismissed Daniel, telling him to go home, something which Daniel obliged to immediately as, even though he'd received such good news, it hadn't woken him up any more than the walk to work had.

Daniel left the restaurant and began the trip back to his dormitory, a constant, small smirk on his face as he thought about just how successful all of the changes had been. Though, he noticed something as he thought about the changes which he'd made. For a while, and he couldn't really recall when it had started, Daniel had started recognising what he needed to change and how he'd do it without fully comprehending that he was still asleep. Everything which was happening to him wasn't happening in the real world. It was all inside of his head, yet, even though he'd acknowledge that occasionally, he hadn't fully processed it. Everything which he was doing was for nothing more than his own satisfaction and contentment. Daniel could see that he was thinking of the new life as more like real life than it was probably healthy to, but he couldn't help it. It was all too realistic.

It made him scared to think about the possibility of him tricking himself in the future into genuinely believing that what was going on was real. What would happen if he'd suddenly wake up within a few years? He'd be thrust back into the miserable life which was *truly* his.

Daniel completed the journey back to his dormitory with the fear that he'd be pulled out of his utopian-like existence and pushed back into his real life. The real life which he wanted to forget so desperately.

Chapter 12

Daniel called out a goodbye to Bryan and Derek as he left the dormitory, Claire with some friends in the city. Elisha had texted him and had asked if they could spend some time together in her dormitory, mainly wanting Daniel to properly meet her three roommates though, apparently, one never slept there and hardly ever spent any time there, with his girlfriend whenever he had the chance, reminding Daniel of how he'd been with Laura.

The request from Elisha had come very suddenly. Originally, he'd been expecting to spend the rest of his Saturday just relaxing on his own or with his roommates, maybe catching up on a small amount of work, not doing too much, though as soon as Elisha had asked the question, Daniel had accepted. It sounded much better than spending most of his time lounging around by himself. Derek and Bryan didn't have long to relax at all, anyway, as they needed to revise for separate exams which happened to take place at the same time.

Elisha's dormitory was on the fourth floor, giving Daniel a fair walk to get there, giving him time to debate how he was going to introduce himself to her roommates. He hadn't met them before at all, not even one of them, didn't even know who she was sharing a

165

dormitory with. Had he met them when he and Elisha were just friends, he wouldn't have felt so nervous though, when thinking about it, Daniel knew that he didn't even *need* to be so nervous. It didn't matter so much if her roommates didn't like him, it only mattered if they didn't *despise* him. If he'd make such a terrible impression which he'd have had to out of his way to do, he'd have a reason to worry, but he knew to just be himself. Nothing would really go wrong with that.

Daniel made it to the stairs, descended them to the fourth floor, then found his way towards Elisha's dormitory. It was the fifth on the left, according to her and, once he'd found the door, he gave a light knock.

After a few moments of waiting, the door opened to reveal Elisha looking very slightly rough, her hair sticking up in places, her face looking slightly grim, though it lit up slightly when she saw Daniel. She pulled him in for a hug, then gave him a quick kiss.

"You okay?" Daniel asked, concerned by her appearance, though Elisha gave a light nod.

"I've just been working since Immunology," she informed him. "I've ended up getting quite stressed, so I thought that you could help me relax."

Daniel followed her to her room, wondering why they were just walking past the living area though, after glancing towards the couches, he saw that no-one was there. So much for his idea of introducing himself.

"Why have you been working for so long?" Daniel questioned, surprised and confused. They stepped into her room and Daniel saw that it was practically the same as his except that it was laid out differently, the bed by the door, her desk and wardrobe across the room, directly opposite the door. "We don't have an exam soon."

"Three weeks," Elisha reminded him, sounding almost stern as if she were indirectly scolding him for not taking his time to revise.

"Yeah, that isn't too close," Daniel insisted, trying to put on a slightly sterner tone, wanting to get across his thoughts that Elisha was pushing herself too much. "We're both two of the best in our classes."

Elisha flashed him a quick, sarcastic-looking glance as she flopped onto her bed, laying down, looking blissful with her head on a pillow. It almost seemed to Daniel as if she was going to fall asleep within moments.

"I'm just scared of failing, that's all," she stated. "I've always gotten really stressed about any sort of exams."

Daniel let out a small, reluctant sigh. He kicked his shoes off, then dropped onto the bed next to her. "I get that," he said. "Just don't push yourself too hard, okay?"

"I can't help it if I do," Elisha replied, her voice sounding slightly distant as if she was trying to fight to remain conscious. She rolled over slightly, closer to Daniel, then propped herself up with her hands, looking at him. "Don't worry about me too much."

"I'll only worry if you give me a reason to worry," Daniel informed her, snarky. He grinned a little and Elisha returned the smile, accepting of his reasoning. She lowered herself a little, close enough to give him a quick kiss before she rolled back to her original position. "So, why did you want me to come here?"

"You don't need to sound so annoyed," she stated sarcastically, glancing at him, suppressing a laugh. "Like I said, I thought it would be easier to unwind with you."

"Depends on what you mean by 'unwind,'" Daniel stated, ignoring Elisha's eye-roll.

"So, is it okay if we spend some time together?" She asked, looking at him, a questioning look on her face as if she was genuinely afraid of Daniel not wanting to spend a few hours with his own girlfriend.

"Of course," Daniel assured, flashing her a small smile. He reached over, pushing his right arm underneath her neck, Elisha sliding a little closer to him. "So, what are we going to do?"

Elisha shrugged. "I was thinking about introducing you to my roommates, but they disappeared when I mentioned it to them," she told him, sounding disappointed.

"I'm not that scary," Daniel joked, Elisha glancing at him, grinning slightly.

"I think they just want to give us some privacy," she told him, sighing slightly, content, though Daniel worried for a second that she was annoyed.

They remained silent for a moment, then Daniel sat up, Elisha following his movements, the two of them leaning against the headboard. "I don't think it's a good idea for us to lay down," Daniel stated simply. "We might fall asleep."

"I wouldn't mind that," Elisha said, leaning her head on Daniel's shoulder before she loosened her muscles and almost collapsed all of her weight into Daniel, leaning into him completely, her arms wrapped around his neck as she clung onto him.

"I suppose I wouldn't, either," Daniel admitted, smirking slightly. He tried his best to look at Elisha, not able to see her face properly, though he liked what he *could* see. She looked peaceful. Her eyes were probably closed, she looked comfortable, she could have even been drifting towards unconsciousness as he looked at her. He wasn't entirely certain, but Daniel wondered slightly if it was a good idea for them to just stay there, fall asleep together, be comfortable. He'd heard that simply sleeping next to a loved one was enough to reduce stress levels even more than just sleeping alone, so it would definitely help Elisha with her issue. Though, at the same time, that would probably give her an incentive to continue working non-stop after waking up. There was the chance that she'd wake up, realise that she wasn't stressed, then continue with her work for hours on end, stress herself out much, much more, then have to repeat the cycle until the distant exam. "Okay, let's do something," Daniel said after a moment of consideration, no activity in mind, though he knew that the two of them staying there wouldn't be very good in the long run.

Elisha raised her head and looked at him, surprised. "What should we do?" She asked, sounding intrigued.

Daniel shrugged a little, almost striking Elisha's chin with his right shoulder. "Not sure," he admitted. "But it's not a good idea to ruin your sleep schedule."

Elisha considered that, then agreed after a moment. "Okay," she said, sounding reluctant, climbing off of the bed before pulling Daniel up. "Let's watch something?"

Daniel gave a small nod, nothing else to suggest in mind.

The two of them spent a while simply sat on Elisha's couch, binge-watching episodes of a TV show which they'd both been watching for a while, having decided to get into a new show together as it would give them a few nice opportunities to discuss something other than themselves and schoolwork.

After two hours of watching the show, the two of Elisha's roommates who actually stayed in the dormitory entered, saw Daniel and Elisha, and immediately introduced themselves.

"I'm Archie," the guy said with a surprisingly deep voice, rushing to Daniel and giving him a quick handshake, having to push his long, frizzy, brown hair out of his eyes afterwards.

"I'm Lizzy," the girl said, staying a few metres away from Daniel, edging towards where must have been her bedroom. She flashed him a smile and started to fiddle with her deep, red hair before silently retreating to her bedroom.

"Where're you going, Lizzy?" Archie asked, turning as she closed her door. "It's rude to ignore a guest!" He called, waiting for her reply.

"It's also rude to interrupt a date!" Lizzy called back with a sing-song voice, a giggle barely audible through the door.

Archie turned back to look at them. "If you're going to do anything, don't do it here," he joked before heading to his room, leaving Elisha to toss a cushion at his back just before the door closed.

"You okay?" Daniel asked Elisha, having noticed that she looked slightly flustered.

"Just a bit much, isn't it?" She muttered, her face having flushed slightly red.

Daniel chuckled. "Well, we've already-"

"Don't," Elisha warned, holding her left index finger in front of Daniel's face, her eyebrows raised, looking slightly intimidating. "I know, but don't say it. It's embarrassing." Her tone completely changed with the last two words, sounding more animated and whinier. Her face even contorted slightly as she pulled her hand away.

Daniel smirked slightly, having spotted an opportunity, something which Elisha recognised too.

"And don't tease me about it," she added quickly, a wide smile on her face which contrasted her tone. She started laughing, then tried to hold it back, possibly imagining the chaos which could come with Daniel teasing her so much, not wanting her laughter to incentivise Daniel to go ahead with the teasing anyway.

Daniel held his hands up. "Okay," he surrendered. "Okay," he repeated, his face blank, defeated.

Elisha waited for a moment to confirm that Daniel wasn't lying, then nodded very slightly. "Good," she stated before, after a moment of hesitation, she leaned into him and un-paused the show.

They stayed there for another hour before Daniel decided that it was time to go. It was approaching six, he was hungry, and he didn't want to intrude for so long. He knew that Elisha wouldn't mind him staying there for longer, obviously, but he wasn't so sure about Archie and Lizzy. They were probably starting to crave food, yet they were confined to their bedrooms out of fear of interfering with Daniel and Elisha.

"I'd better go, then," Daniel let out suddenly a few moments after they'd finished an episode. It was slow, luckily, so he wasn't going to force the two of them to leave the show in the middle of an intense moment.

"Really?" Elisha questioned, sounding disappointed. She raised her head from his shoulder and gave him an expression which was similar to what Laura used to give Daniel whenever she'd want something. "Now?"

"Yeah," Daniel said. "I have some work to do, I'd better eat, you know."

Elisha looked slightly disappointed but understanding. "Okay," she said, standing up.

172

Daniel stood, too. "Don't overdo it," he instructed, starting to walk towards the door, Elisha following by his side.

"I won't," she said, sounding slightly fed-up. She probably didn't like to think that Daniel was so worried about her.

Daniel pulled the door open, went to step outside, then was pulled back and into a tight embrace.

"I love you," Elisha told him, pulling her head away for a moment to give him a lengthened kiss.

"I-I love you, too," Daniel spluttered, out of breath once they'd parted.

Elisha smiled, looking slightly shy and joyous before she stepped back, giving Daniel enough space to leave the dormitory.

"I'll see you tomorrow?" She asked as Daniel turned around, avoiding someone whom he didn't know as they passed in front of the dormitory. "Monday?"

"Probably Monday," Daniel told her, not liking that idea, but he had a shift the next day and had to finish a project off for Virology, probably one of the things which Elisha had been stressing over.

"Okay," Elisha said, smiling, not sounding too down about it as she understood that it couldn't be helped. She stepped forwards and gave Daniel another kiss, quick this time, pulling away after a few milliseconds.

"See ya," Daniel let out before he turned and walked away from the dormitory, heading towards the stairs, starting to think about what he'd make for everyone for dinner. They rotated who was cooking each night and, as it turned out, it was Daniel's turn to make something, one of the main reasons as to why he didn't want to stay with Elisha for much longer.

Daniel ascended the stairs while deciding between a few choices of meals, jumping between the idea of a stir fry and spaghetti the most, eventually landing on the idea of a stir fry before he heard a commotion above him.

Once Daniel made it to his floor, he caught sight of Laura ahead of him, prancing towards her dormitory, her right arm wrapped around the waist of a guy whom Daniel didn't know, her hand in his right, front pocket.

Daniel paused for a moment upon seeing the sight, then made an effort to hide around the corner, waiting for Laura and her possible new boyfriend to enter her dormitory before he stepped out and continued heading towards his own dormitory.

Good luck, mate, Daniel thought grimly, wondering for a moment if it was a good idea to warn the guy about what Laura was like, though he ruled it out. *It's not my life*, he told himself nonchalantly.

Daniel paused a few steps away from his door, thinking. "I'm not bothered," he whispered to himself, surprised. He didn't care that Laura was with someone else. Why? He'd gotten over Laura before, at least probably, and he'd recognised that early on, a month or two before, but still. Wouldn't it hurt, usually? Even though Daniel didn't have a desire to get back together with Laura, shouldn't it hurt to see her with someone else, practically frisking him in the hallway, all lovey-dovey as she'd once been with him? Maybe it was the fact that she'd been cheating on him, having given Daniel the pain of seeing her with someone else already, or maybe it was because *he* was dating someone else already, but Daniel could tell for certain that he didn't care. "I don't care," he whispered to himself, surprised and happy about that fact. "I don't care," he repeated.

Daniel walked into his dormitory, buzzing about his discovery.

Chapter 13

The final exams were nearing at a pace which Daniel was slightly used to, having lived through the experience before, though, now, he didn't feel as overwhelmed or as petrified as before. When it came to work, he hadn't been slacking, something which was a massive change. If anything, he'd made such an effort to make sure that he *wasn't* going to fall behind that he'd practically *over*-revised, everything more or less already cemented in his mind. Everybody else, Elisha and Derek, mainly, were finding it very difficult to keep up with everything, having resulted in Daniel taking initiative and organising revision sessions. He and Elisha were revising together three times a week after their school days while Derek and somebody else who was taking the same course as he was were working together. Bryan and Claire, as far as Daniel knew, were barely managing. He'd suggested the same concept to both of them, though they'd declined, saying that they simply couldn't revise with another person as they'd just end up becoming distracted.

Daniel, Elisha, Derek, Claire and Bryan were sat in Daniel's dormitory in the living area, split up over the two couches, the five of them having decided to relax for a change and spend their time together to do so.

176

They'd originally expected to just watch something on the TV, though they'd ended up becoming roped-up in a conversation regarding the exams, something which wasn't exactly ideal when it came to their stress levels.

"I'm just so nervous," Derek muttered, leaning forwards, his hands clasped together as he stared at the ground. "I don't want to fail and ruin everything which I've been working towards."

"Yeah, I know how bad it is," Daniel barely muttered though, Elisha, who was sat on his knee, leaning into the back of the couch, heard him and gave him an odd look.

"There's not much to worry about, right?" Claire assured, sounding slightly unsure but hopeful. "We just need to make sure that we know what we're talking about. It's just the same as all of the other exams which we've taken."

"Just with more on the line," Bryan reminded her, to which Claire gave him a scathing look for bringing the mood down again.

They all went quiet for a moment, something which was probably slightly unhealthy as they were all undoubtedly, except for Daniel, thinking about the building stress.

"We'll be fine," Daniel stated after a moment, not liking the atmosphere in the room. "Claire's right, we just need to revise enough, and we're all doing that, so…"

"Well, what if we forget something in the exam?" Elisha questioned, wincing after she spoke as if immediately regretting that she'd said anything in the first place.

"Then we'll pass by answering all of the other questions correctly," Daniel assured her, hoping that it would be the case. "We're all smart."

"Except for Derek," Claire added quickly, glancing at Derek with a grin, though he didn't seem to appreciate the joke very much.

"Yeah, thanks for that," he spat, not looking up from the floor.

"We'll be fine," Bryan interjected, giving Daniel a look which made it seem as if he was questioning whether Daniel was correct despite agreeing with him.

"Yeah," Elisha agreed after a moment, nodding lightly as if still trying to convince herself that she *would* be okay.

"Yeah, I guess," Claire mumbled after a moment of consideration, then she shook her head. "We need to stop thinking like this," she stated suddenly. "We'll be *fine*," she assured, emphasising the last word. "We just need to take it as it happens."

Everyone nodded unanimously as if they were part of a play, quieting until Elisha decided to change the topic and distract everyone from their doubts, whether they were prominent or muffled, starting a conversation which Daniel didn't bother to pay attention to. One thing was on his mind, something which he'd realised a few days before: he wasn't nervous at all. He wasn't scared about the upcoming exams, he wasn't worried that he was going to fail again. He'd been doing

178

so much over the time which he'd spent in his lucid dream simply trying to ensure that he *wouldn't* fail, no matter what would happen. Maybe it was the fact that, if he really wanted to, Daniel could cheat the examination a little, make it so that all of the questions would be really easy or that the grade boundaries would be so low that anyone simply guessing all of the answers would be able to get an A. Daniel knew that he didn't want to cheat the exam, whether with a traditional method or not, but that didn't make him feel nervous in the slightest. He didn't really care that his entire dream was leading up the moment where he'd sit at the table, stare at the paper in front of him and open it to look at the first page. It was almost as if he *knew* that he'd pass.

Where had the confidence come from? That was something which Daniel had no idea how to even begin figuring out. He didn't have the confidence the first time around as he hadn't been prepared but, now, he was. Was that it? Was he confident only because he was prepared? Or, at the very least, because he *thought* that he was?

"We should *actually* relax, right?" Bryan said after a moment, pulling everybody away from their thoughts. Daniel knew that he was the only one in the room worrying about the fact that he wasn't worried about the exams. He knew that the others would kill for that privilege, yet it made him feel uncomfortable.

"Yeah," Derek grunted, looking up for the first time in a few minutes. He stared at the TV screen. "Game?"

"Film?" Claire countered.

"Those in favour of a game," Derek said, holding his hand up. Bryan and Daniel followed suit before, after a moment, Elisha joined.

Claire rolled her eyes slightly. "Okay, your honour," she grumbled, though her tone had a tinge of amusement behind it.

Derek spent a moment setting a game up on one of the few consoles which resided by the TV while everyone watched or, at least, *appeared* to have been watching, more likely thinking about something.

Daniel stood up, having to slide Elisha from his knee and onto the arm of the couch. "Just going to the bathroom," he informed, ignoring the silence which followed.

He walked to the bathroom, closed the door, then stared at himself in the mirror. Not being nervous and having so much confidence in himself was enough to confuse him and worry him, ironically enough. Staring at himself, staring deep into his own eyes, Daniel tried to see if he could figure out the reason. Then it clicked. He wasn't nervous because he didn't have a reason to be nervous. It was his dream. He was asleep. Everything in this reality was playing by *his* rules. He didn't feel nervous because he didn't *want* to feel nervous. Then, would it be a good idea to stop the others from feeling their nerves? Or would that be meddling too much? To Daniel, it seemed slightly inhumane to toy with other people's emotions by switching them on or off as if each feeling was a light switch, but would it

180

hurt to try? He hadn't tried to do anything which affecting anybody else except him. Well, except for Austin, but he hadn't been breaking the rules of reality for that. Daniel hadn't changed something huge just to get his way. Would it be so bad to just try something small and see if he could do it? Maybe it would turn out that his own brain was putting restrictions on itself. Maybe he wouldn't be able to do anything like that.

I don't want Elisha to be nervous, Daniel thought to himself as he moved to lean on the sink. He stared at the basin, closed his eyes tight, then tried to picture the words in his mind. *I don't want Elisha to be nervous* was almost ingrained on the inside of his eyelids. He couldn't escape the sight of those colourless, shapeless words no matter what part of his eyelids he tried to focus on. They were simply a constant, consistently there, always there no matter what.

Daniel opened his eyes and blinked a few times, his eyesight compromised and dimmer than usual until, after a few moments, it faded back to normal.

"Right," Daniel muttered to himself. "Let's see if that's done anything."

Daniel flushed the toilet, not wanting it to seem weird for him to have simply entered and left the bathroom needlessly before he opened the door. Elisha was stood right there, waiting for him as if he'd called for her.

She flashed a quick smile, then hugged him, then dragged him back to the others. Claire was staring at the coffee table, kicking her legs back and forth slightly, her calves making dull thuds against the couch, Bryan was fiddling with his fingers as he usually did when he was bored, and Derek had just finished setting everything up.

Elisha pushed Daniel onto the couch in a playful manner, taking a moment to wait for him to sit up properly before she dropped onto his lap and returned to her previous position, watching Derek as he moved back to the couch, trying to juggle four controllers.

"Only have four," he stated, handing one to Bryan, one to Claire, then held one towards Daniel and Elisha.

"I'll sit this one out," Daniel told him, tilting his head towards Elisha before Derek held it to her and she took it.

Derek dropped back onto the couch and started setting a game up for everyone while Daniel stared at the side of Elisha's face. She'd definitely changed. Daniel knew that he'd managed to change *something*, though he didn't know if he'd only eliminated her nervousness.

"Nervous?" Daniel grumbled to her, pulling on her left shoulder to make her lean closer to him, wanting to talk quietly, not wishing to remind the others about their worries.

Elisha looked at him, her face blank. She shook her head very slightly. "No, not anymore," she replied, then her face dropped and she looked perplexed. "That's… weird," she muttered.

Daniel shrugged. "You must have just realised

that you're the smartest girl I know," he whispered, then kissed her on the cheek quickly, wanting to pass the moment off as if he'd just wanted to be sweet.

Elisha grinned, kissed him on the forehead, then turned her attention back to the TV screen, holding the controller at the ready as Derek was about to start a multiplayer game.

Daniel tried to think rationally about the situation for a few moments, but a barrage of sudden thoughts overwhelmed him. He had a lot of power. A *serious* amount of power. What if he'd been using that power the whole time? What if he'd *made* Laura cheat on him again because he'd been thinking about how she'd cheated on him in real life when he saw her? What if he'd only possibly stopped Austin's death because he simply didn't *want* Austin to die, not because he'd managed to come up with a plan which had saved his life? What if he hadn't *earned* his job this time, but he'd been employed because he'd *wanted* the job? What if he hadn't *earned* the promotion either, but had simply been given one as he'd thought about the possibility earlier in the day? What if he and Elisha had gotten together because, deep down, even if he hadn't realised it at the time, he'd loved her? What if he hadn't been doing well in school, but he'd just been getting good marks because he *wanted* to pass? It wasn't unreasonable to think along those lines. He *had* just stopped Elisha from feeling nervous simply because he'd *wanted* her to feel okay. If craving something was enough to make it come true, did that mean that everything which he'd changed, everything which he'd experienced, had all come as a result of him *urging* it subconsciously?

Daniel let out a shaky breath, then quickly blinked a few times. *I want to stop thinking about this,* he pleaded to himself. *Stop! Stop! Stop!*

Daniel looked up and felt enticed by the game on the screen.

Chapter 14

The graduation hall was impeccably large, grand and expensive-looking. Daniel stared at it in awe from the entrance, stood just in front of the doorway with Elisha and Derek to either side of him.

"It's amazing," Elisha breathed, taking a step forwards, nearly stepping on a slither of her black, slightly-oversized gown, jolting backwards to avoid doing so before she returned her gaze to the room, still stunned.

Daniel couldn't help but gape at the sight. There were long, ceremonial rows of seats which somehow looked magnificent despite the fact that they were plain chairs. Everything was lit up by a ginormous chandelier which clung to the peaking roof with a long, golden chain, candles mounted on the walls to cover the shadows with a flickering light from their flames. Above them were extra seats, almost like a theatre, all four sides of what would have been the third storey with another seating area which sloped towards the centre where, underneath, resided a gigantic, square, black and glossy stage with a podium and a microphone. Everything from the barriers which separated the elevated seating from the drop to the pattern on the floor was immaculate and, as Daniel saw it, perfectly fitting for a ceremony. It was perfect for a university graduation.

Everyone was ushered towards seating which resided as close to the stage as possible. Once seated, everybody who was graduating made a square ring around the outside of the stage, not a single extra seat to ruin the aesthetic, not even an extra person who had to have been seated behind somebody else. It was as if the seating arrangements had been calculated to precisely fit everybody without a single detail amiss.

Daniel sat with Elisha to his left, Derek to his right, Claire on the other side of Derek and Bryan on the other side of Elisha. The five of them were sat together as if they were playing the main characters of a movie, all sat at the premiere for the film in the front row.

"I can't believe it's finally happening," Elisha let out, to which Daniel smirked and Bryan rolled his eyes slightly.

"That's the third time you've said that today," Bryan counted, holding up three fingers as if his right hand was a tally which was constantly being updated.

"I know, I know," Elisha assured. "It's just insane!"

"And that's the second time that you've said *that*," Daniel added, grinning as he stared at her, then glanced at Bryan, the two of them exchanging amused looks.

Elisha lightly pushed Daniel and Bryan simultaneously, both of them bouncing back and nudging her before they stilled and returned to their

186

awe-filled gazes of the hall.

Daniel couldn't think of a word to describe the area which wasn't "beautiful" or "perfect." His mind was simply struggling to come up with anything else as his eyes struggled to take in everything around him. There were just too many details to focus on. The bright, blinding white of the marble candle holders, the frost-coloured, zig-zag patterned floor, the walls which jutted in and out in places, pillars which didn't look to be holding anything up, pillars which were supporting the elevated seating, all of the banisters and barricades, everything tinted which had a dark, gold shade, teetering between the appearance of a royal's throne room and a traditional church. The only things which were missing were the constant reminders of Christianity.

A stampede of footsteps came from the doors, prompting each graduating student to gaze at the sight of their families all walking in, dressed as if they were visiting the Queen of England, everybody looking magnificent, gazing at their relatives with glee as they headed to their seats.

Daniel didn't catch a sight of his family at first, guessing that they were being obscured by everybody else, but saw his mother, father, aunt and grandmother after a few moments, the four of them fairly far away from him on the other side of the stage, not too far from the door.

"It's weird, isn't it?" Derek asked rhetorically, staring at the crowd ahead of them, searching for his family before he gave up on that section and turned to look everywhere else. "We've all been working so hard for this for literally all of our lives, and in a few hours, the whole experience will just be a collection of memories," he finished, spotting his family as he finished talking, giving them a quick, enthusiastic wave.

"Since when have you been so…" Claire began, struggling to find a word to describe Derek's revelation. "I don't know."

Derek shrugged. "Must just be the cusp of adulthood talking," he guessed, pulling a slightly amused face as he realised that he was speaking as if he was forcing a change in his personality very slightly.

More and more people continued to file into the magnificent hall, people beginning to fill up the seats on the ground level. After a few minutes, people began heading towards two, grand staircases which resided against the walls to the right and left, leading to the elevated seating area, those seats beginning to fill, too. After what must have only been a couple of minutes, people stopped entering, Daniel guessing that everyone had arrived.

A few moments of complete silence passed before the chancellor of the university stepped onto the stage, having emerged from somewhere in the crowd. He waltzed towards the microphone stand, pulled the microphone from the stand, then took a moment to look over everybody, appearing gleeful.

"I'd like to say that everybody graduating tonight deserves the honour of receiving their degrees

188

or their PhDs," he said, his deeper voice booming throughout the hall, echoing everywhere, conjuring a strangely cosy atmosphere. "As the chancellor, I've seen these people grow from enthusiastic and ambitious students to the depressed adults whom we know today," he said, making everybody laugh. He suppressed a chuckle of his own before continuing. "The people whom we're celebrating for tonight have spent years of their lives working laboriously for this very moment, and I believe that they all deserve a round of applause."

The hall became almost like a theatre, everybody beginning to clap for each other within a few moments as if they'd just finished watching a terrific, indescribable performance. Everybody applauded for the graduates and, while Daniel knew that the applause wasn't only for him, he felt slightly as if his efforts and his previous suffering was being recognised.

It took a few moments for everybody to calm down and to allow the chancellor to continue speaking. "I consider it an honour every day that I get to watch people discover what they're passionate about and that I get to see people mature into well-rounded humans," he continued, making everybody go quiet as they paid as close attention to him as possible. "Everybody graduating tonight has worked incredibly hard just for this moment, I couldn't be prouder of each of them."

Everybody began applauding the chancellor after a moment of silence as he signified that his speech had come to an end. He placed the microphone back onto its stand, took a few steps away from the

189

microphone and joined in, applauding the graduates instead of himself before he stepped closer to the microphone again. "Now, miss Kayleigh Leonard would like to say a few words."

The chancellor gestured towards a young-looking Korean girl whom Daniel didn't recognise, motioning for her to step onto the stage. She did so fairly quickly, people applauding her for simply standing on the platform. She walked towards the microphone as the chancellor dropped off of the stage and sat down in the audience, close to the front.

"Hello," the girl let out, her voice slightly shaky. She was clearly nervous, but she also looked tremendously excited. "I've been enrolled in this university for five years," she began. "Every day, no matter what I was facing, I've felt welcome and at home, and that's something which I'm incredibly grateful for. The professors, all of the staff, made an effort to make sure that I wasn't falling behind with my work, they made sure that I wasn't feeling overwhelmed. There was a time in my third year where I started to feel very stressed, but every effort was taken to ensure that I had some time to relax."

Daniel stared at the girl, wondering why the speech was jumping out to him as if he was the one saying the words, as if everything which the girl was saying was being pulled from his head.

"Every day has been an adventure with its ups and downs, and even though I've occasionally felt as if dropping out would have been the best option, I made sure to stick to it. I'm incredibly pleased with myself for making that decision. Being stood here today in front of all of you, people whom I don't even know, people whom I've never seen in my life, I feel as if everyone is cheering me on."

Kayleigh turned around with the microphone in hand, looking in every direction at everybody in the audience, possibly not wanting anybody to feel as if she wasn't talking to them.

"For every step of the way, I've had people looking out for me," she continued. "Though every moment which felt like the end of my life, I've had my friends, the professors, everybody making sure that I was okay."

She turned a little again, facing away from Daniel completely, though it felt to him as if she was staring at him and reciting what was running through his mind.

"Some people come out of university and feel happy that they don't have to deal with the stress anymore, some people come out of university and feel upset as they're leaving behind what they've been used to for however long." She paused and gazed at a few different people in the audience, maybe people whom she knew and was referring to. "But I feel glad that I've had such an amazing experience. I feel joyous to be able to say that I've been able to experience the best five years of my life, and I'm excited to see what the future holds. I'm intrigued as to what's going to face me in the future. I'm nervous, of course, but I'm more excited than anything else."

Kayleigh turned again, took a deep breath, and looked right at Daniel. "Some people in this hall may feel completely lost or entirely satisfied," she looked away from Daniel, "but I can safely say that everybody's grateful for the experience."

Kayleigh went quiet and the hall burst into applause once more, causing a grin to form on her face before she placed the microphone back into its stand and returned to her seat.

There was silence for a few moments, everyone having a chance to maul over the words which had been presented by Kayleigh. Daniel sat in a stunned stupor for a few moments before he realised that the chancellor was returning to stage, swiftly returning his attention to what was going on around him.

"Thank you, Kayleigh," the chancellor said, smiling. "Now, before we get to the ceremony, as per tradition, we have a lovely choir to grace us with their beautiful voices," he said, a slurry of people beginning to file onto the stage behind him, facing in all four directions, the shape somewhere between a circle and a square.

The choir continued to spill onto the stage as people began applauding for them, the chancellor leaving and the applause ceasing once the choir was entirely on the stage, shaped like a square with rounded corners.

There was a moment of silence before the choir began to chant their song.

Daniel immediately felt drawn away from the performance, the strangeness of how Kayleigh's speech had related to him so much keeping him distracted. He genuinely felt as if she'd been talking directly to him for the entire time, presenting him with his own feelings, his own mindset. It was as if she'd been looking right through him, into his mind, spilling everything out for everybody else to hear. Daniel guessed that it could have been his mind's way of reminding him that everything which he was experiencing was fake and that it was glorified just for his experience, though Daniel wasn't completely certain. It could have simply been plucked from his mind for the sole reason that relating to the speech given by a graduate would make the ceremony even more special for him, even if the speech seemed much shorter than usual speeches. Everything had simply been presented as it was with nothing to sugar-coat it. That was what, to Daniel, *really* made it seem as if it had been his brain serving him his own feelings and thoughts.

A high note sung by a young boy in the choir jolted Daniel from his thoughts, snapping him back to what was going on, though he quickly started to feel the grasp of his thoughts pulling at him, having to struggle to keep himself in the moment.

The choir sang for two minutes though, to Daniel, it felt as if it was taking at least ten as he struggled, not wanting to be pulled away from the moment. It wasn't the time to debate with himself about certain events. He was graduating! Finally! He was in the moment which he'd been anticipating for years, and the moment which he'd previously missed out on and sorely regretted missing. He was finally graduating, so why let anything distract him from the momentous occasion?

The hall burst into applause yet again once the choir had finished, the chancellor promptly rushing onto the stage alongside the vice-chancellor, the two of them grinning wildly. The vice-chancellor held a giant cluster of graduation certificates alongside the PhDs or degrees which had been earned, being extremely careful as to not drop them.

"Now," the chancellor began, clapping his hands together lightly which, once having been picked up by the microphone, sounded more like a sharp snap than anything else. "We'll call out the names of everybody graduating, and with every student, we'd love for you all to join in with congratulating them for their efforts," he explained, giving a stiff nod afterwards before stepping back slightly, allowing for the vice-chancellor to stand close-enough to the microphone for her voice to be picked up.

The vice-chancellor began calling out names, people walking onto the stage with applause in the background as they headed to the chancellor to collect their certificate and degree which had been handed to him, shaking the hands of the two of them before walking off of the stage on the other side and finding their way back to their seat. Plenty of people collected their awards, some of whom Daniel recognised, some whom he didn't. One such person was, as it happened, the boy whom Laura had cheated on Daniel with, something which surprised Daniel as being with her had been the sole reason why he hadn't had a chance to earn his PhD in the first place.

It took a few minutes for someone whom Daniel knew well to have their name called: Claire. She waltzed onto the stage, looking gleeful. She took her award and certificate, shook the hand of the chancellor and vice-chancellor, then left the stage while staring at the two things in her hands, overjoyed, clearly. Daniel, Bryan, Elisha and Derek congratulated her once she'd returned to her seat, Derek looking at the certificate which she held, interested in the design.

After another few moments, Bryan was called. He went through the same process, taking his awards, shaking their hands then, after leaving the stage and while on his way back to his seat, Daniel saw him duck towards somebody else quickly, kissing him before pulling away, looking even happier, somehow. The crowd almost cheered at the sight, something which drew the complete attention of Daniel, Elisha, Derek and Claire. As the four of them watched, they could only guess that the man whom Bryan had kissed was Jacob, the four of them making an effort to see what he looked like though, unfortunately, they didn't get much of a look.

Once Bryan had returned, Elisha made a point of pestering him quietly, demanding to know if that was Jacob. Bryan's face went red and he went quiet, embarrassed, refusing to answer any question regarding the moment.

A few more people were called onto the stage, including Derek. He simply followed the procedure like everyone else, not doing anything to stand out, returning to his seat within a few moments, staring at the certificate, then at the PhD, then at the certificate, then at the PhD.

Daniel couldn't take his eyes off of the PhD in Derek's hands, almost fascinated by it. He was going to own one of those! Finally, after doing so much work to get one!

More people received their awards, then Elisha did. She walked onto the stage, almost shaking a little from the excitement. Daniel could see her hands shaking slightly as she took the certificate and the PhD from the chancellor and, for a moment, Daniel almost believed that she was cold.

Elisha left the stage and returned to her seat, still buzzing slightly, a wide smile on her face which Daniel thought almost looked too wide to have been real.

"Congratulations," Daniel whispered to her, looking her in the eyes, amused by how gleeful she was, but also slightly impatient as he wanted to feel the same joy.

"Thanks," she whispered back, giving him a quick kiss before she turned and stared at the PhD, her eyes wide and her pupils dilated slightly. Daniel could tell just how proud she was of herself, something which she definitely deserved as, for what must have been at least two months, she'd been experiencing rapidly fluctuating waves of stress which would either cause her to be too scared to do anything except for working or which would make her break down a little. She'd been through what had probably felt like hell.

One more person was called before Daniel was. He stood up shakily and started advancing towards the steps to the stage, climbing on, each step making his heart beat faster and faster.

"Congratulations, Daniel," the chancellor let out once the two of them were close enough to talk properly. He handed the PhD and the certificate to Daniel with his left hand and held his right hand out for Daniel to shake.

Daniel took the awards with his left hand, shook the chancellor's hand, then the vice-chancellor's hand, before walking off of the stage to the sound of applause which made him feel as if he'd just solved major problems in the world and was being hailed as a king by the masses of people on Earth. He felt on top of the world. His heart was beating so fast that Daniel could feel the pressure in his ears and eyes rising. His hands were slightly sweaty, his pace was quickened, his eyes were darting around everywhere, taking in the crowd surrounding him as he walked down the stairs and made his way back to his friends.

After taking his seat, everyone congratulated him, Elisha gave him another quick kiss, then Daniel spent the rest of the ceremony simply staring at the awards in his hands.

Once the names had stopped being called, the

vice-chancellor stepped off of the stage while the chancellor approached the microphone. He paused for a moment before opening his mouth to speak. "To everybody graduating: good luck!" He let out. "Now, go and celebrate with everyone! You're officially graduates!"

Everybody cheered, some more over-enthusiastic than others. Daniel felt as if the energy in the room wouldn't ever have had a chance of being matched or beaten. Everybody was so overjoyed with themselves, with their friends, with their families that they could only let it out with a unified roar of triumph.

It took a few moments for everybody to calm down and for everybody to begin filing out of the building, the guests leaving first, the graduates staying where they were for a moment, rushing around to find their friends if they weren't sat with them.

"Well, that's that," Derek let out, to which Claire nudged him lightly.

"Could you be any less happy?" She asked jokingly, a giant grin on her face. She stepped in front of everyone and looked them over. "I can't believe that this is it."

"Yeah, we're officially adults, I guess," Bryan said.

"That happened a while ago," Elisha interjected, shrugging lightly, seeing where Bryan was coming from but not agreeing entirely.

"Well, whatever you want to say, we've finished the journey," Derek summarised, giving a light shrug of his own, breaking into a chuckle.

"Yeah," Daniel muttered to himself, looking down at the PhD in his hands, the certificate held behind it. "The long, tiring journey."

The five of them pulled each other in for a giant group hug, cherishing the moment while it lasted, knowing that it was going to be the last time that they'd all be together with the overwhelming joy of having just graduating from university. Daniel knew that they had to separate at some point, but that didn't mean that he didn't have the urge to cling to the people who had helped him through his long and confusing battle.

The five of them disbanded and, after taking a moment to look each other over, they all walked out of the hall together, heading towards the exit, prepared for the beginning of their new lives.

Chapter 15

Daniel opened his eyes slowly as he stretched his arm towards his bedside table, turning the alarm off, feeling the chilly air within the room. For a moment, he felt a very strange feeling in his stomach, almost as if he was nervous for some reason. Then a very sudden wave of intense fear rushed over him.

Daniel realised after a moment of laying and thinking about it, struggling to find the reason as to why he felt so worried, that he'd had a very strange dream which had mixed memories and fabricated events, one which was at the brink of being forgotten, though it hadn't quite reached the point of total obscurity. Daniel could recall that he'd been thrusted into a life which hadn't been very pleasant to him. His girlfriend, Laura, had confessed that she'd stopped loving him long before and had confessed that she'd been cheating on him for a long time, too. On top of that, not only had Daniel been blamed for something which didn't have anything to do with him and, as a result, had been fired, but his family cat of many years had also been struck by a car and had been killed. Then, while on his way back from a walk which he'd decided would clear his mind, he'd witnessed a motorbike accident which had resulted in the death of the rider and the possible death of the two people whom the bike had struck.

After having returned to his apartment, Daniel had fallen into what he had believed within the dream to have been a lucid dream of its own. That dream had taken him back to his last year of university and had fabricated a collection of terrible events which had never happened to begin with. Daniel, however, didn't know that, having believed that they'd really happened, and had fought to change the outcome of all of those events, eventually having gotten himself to where he was laying. Or, maybe, those events *had* happened and he *had* changed things. Maybe the beginning of the dream had been the memories and the rest had been the fabrication. Daniel couldn't tell which was which, leading him to two possibilities: either he'd changed the past or he was… still dreaming.

Daniel gulped upon that last thought, scared, worried that he was still dreaming and that everything which he'd lived through, everything which he'd worked so hard for, had been a lie. But no, that wasn't possible, surely. He felt awake. So…

Daniel had changed the past.

He knew it within an instant. He was awake. He was definitely awake, and a wave of memories came flooding back to him. Seeing Laura cheating on him in university. How he and Elisha had met. The party which had forced romantic tension between the two of them. Seeing Austin on the day before he was due to die. Stopping himself from being fired from his job as a waiter in a restaurant. Ensuring that he gained his PhD.

He'd changed the past. Daniel could remember, vividly remember upon thinking about it, that he'd lived through his last year of university *twice*. One would have been within a dream, the other within reality, and Daniel knew that he wasn't dreaming. He even pinched his arm and felt the corresponding pain. He wasn't asleep, meaning that everything from the beginning of the dream was reality? Or, *had* been reality? He'd really experienced that? The lucid dream which he'd fallen into had been where he'd changed the past then, remembering what had happened the first time around, ensuring that he wouldn't make the same mistakes as he did?

Daniel let out a shaky breath, then held a hand to his forehead. It was a lot to take in and way too much to try to comprehend, especially given that the thoughts had suddenly burst into his mind with no clear reason. He'd simply woken up, had felt strange, then had been bombarded with these… ideas. The only thing which Daniel was certain about was that he was *awake*. To remember everything about the weird, time-shifting dream which he'd had meant that he was awake, right? Therefore, Daniel concluded, he was awake and he'd changed the past.

Daniel decided the leave the thought there and move on as if nothing had happened.

After craning his neck to look at Elisha as best as possible, Daniel gave Elisha a light kiss on the head. It was her day off, so he wasn't going to wake her up.

Daniel, as carefully as possible, slid away from

Elisha, moving her head so that it was resting on the pillow. Once he was out of the bed, he smiled at the sight of her, then grabbed some clean clothes and walked into the en suite bathroom.

After closing the door and turning the shower on to let it warm up properly, Daniel quickly used the toilet, brushed his teeth, then shaved with an electric razor, leaving a thin layer of stubble on his face before he climbed into the shower.

Three years had passed since Daniel, Elisha, Claire, Bryan and Derek had graduated from university, and they'd all been very lucky. Daniel and Elisha had both received internships at the same laboratory not too long after graduating and, after having been taught the ropes properly, they were hired full-time. Of course, Daniel had to leave his job at the restaurant, though everybody there had been incredibly supportive and there hadn't been any unnecessary tension between Daniel and Dale. Daniel had already trained a decent few waiters, having also trained one or two to have the capabilities to train others, so he wasn't leaving the place in shambles without him there to lead the other waiters. Someone was able to take over right away.

Derek, Bryan and Claire had also had a decent portion of luck, the three of them entering their desired fields. Bryan had also finally introduced them all to Jacob, something which had ended up being incredibly exciting for everybody as he'd gone for however long without letting the secret of Jacob's identity out.

Daniel lathered his short and tidy hair with

shampoo thoroughly before washing it out, moving to wash his face properly.

He and Elisha were engaged. Daniel had proposed to her a few months earlier incredibly simply during a date night which they'd spent at their own house. He'd pretended to have lost something and had the two of them searching for the lost object, getting onto one knee with the ring in his hand while Elisha had her back turned. He could picture the look of surprise and then glee which she'd had on her face whenever he wanted, having cemented the image in his mind, occasionally gazing at it whenever he was feeling down about anything. It never failed to cheer him up.

Austin had survived, too. Daniel's plan had worked, having postponed Austin's morning schedule enough to have almost made him late for work. Daniel had received a call from Austin not long after having graduated from university. He'd wanted to catch-up with Daniel and to spend another day together, just hanging out, and Daniel had found out that Austin had finally quit his job at the clothing-store and that he'd managed to move on to being the manager of a local fast-food restaurant. He'd also gotten engaged, like Daniel, and was due to be married within a month or two.

Daniel finished washing his face before he moved to begin washing his body, whistling to a song which has been stuck in his head for days, one which he'd heard on the radio in passing but hadn't heard the name of and hadn't been able to make sense of the lyrics, something which had been incredibly unfortunate as he'd had no way of finding out what the song was and, therefore, couldn't silence the earworm by listening to the tune.

Daniel turned the shower off, climbed out, then began to dry himself, doing his best to be as thorough as possible before pulling his clothes on and using the towel the vigorously shake the water from his hair, drying it as best as possible, not wanting to use the hairdryer out of fear of waking Elisha up.

After a few moments, Daniel walked out of the bathroom, found that Elisha was still asleep, and made sure to creep out of the room, closing the door behind him quietly before he went down the stairs and headed to the kitchen to get breakfast.

While Daniel waited for his toast, he used his phone to check the news and saw that Gregory Flynn had apparently started acting, having played a major role in a film. Gregory was one of Derek's friends, someone who'd dropped out of university fairly early-on, though he'd kept contact with Derek regardless. Daniel had met him once. Gregory seemed like a decent guy, so Daniel was happy for him that he was getting out there even more on top of his crazily-popular online therapy sessions which he held.

Daniel's toast popped up. He grabbed it from the toaster, slathered some butter onto it, then immediately began eating. He only had a few minutes before he had to leave for work, so he didn't want to bother with getting a plate for a single piece of toast.

While eating, Daniel grabbed everything which he needed and left the house, locking the door behind him just in case even though Elisha was still there before he climbed into his car, just finishing the piece of toast as he did so.

Daniel started the car engine and, while backing out of the driveway, thought back to his worries from before. He was awake, wasn't he? Daniel suddenly felt slightly unsure and so, just to prove it to himself, Daniel stamped on his left foot as hard as possible.

The pain which Daniel felt assured him that he was awake, putting the fear in his mind to rest. He was awake and he'd changed the past, somehow. For some reason, Daniel felt slightly blasé about it, though he acknowledged that it would definitely be worth it to look into the strange phenomenon more in depth. Maybe that's what he'd do that day.

Daniel began the drive to the laboratory which he worked at, a tinge of worry still present in his mind, though he refused to acknowledge it.

Printed in Great Britain
by Amazon

59819744R00122